Jim was a loving father in a rocky marriage. His life was simple: work, love his daughter and try to keep his family together. All of that would change in a matter of five minutes. Now with his wife gone, his daughter murdered and him in prison, Jim's mind and will to live is all but gone. As events unfold Jim's will and mind return, but in a twisted state. When he is faced with the truth of what destroyed his life, will he snap? And will he be justified in doing so?

2

Justified

4

Cover design by Jacobe Noonan
Edited by Charita Moore

ISBN: 978-0-6151-5121-2

Printed in the United States of America

Acknowledgements

First, I would like to thank God for blessing me with life, a wonderful imagination and a family that would make me want to write about a man going insane. But seriously, thank you God for life and the strength to complete this.

I'd like to thank Ashley Flemming for inspiring me to write a book. Even though she started to write her book first and I finished before she did.

I'd like to thank Charita Moore for editing the book. So if there are any errors, I'm blaming her.

I'd like to thank Jacobe Noonan for a wonderful job on the cover. Best work I've ever seen, hands down.

I'd like to thank all the people who read the book and gave me honest input. Thanks Carita, Wanda and Ashley.

I'd like to thank me for writing the book, thanks me!

And I would just like to thank Lulu Publishing for being such a brilliant website and giving authors like me the opportunity to have our voices heard.

1

"Five minutes," I shouted up the stairs, as I grabbed my coat and keys and headed for the door.

"I'm coming!" Emily yelled down.

It was the same thing every morning. We had to be out of the door at 7:30am and she was always late.

Crystal came running down the stairs. "I'm ready daddy."

"I know, baby."

Daddy. I loved it when she called me that. I remember the first time she looked at me and said the most wonderful word in the English language. I remember walking into the kitchen, and with her shirt covered with spaghetti, she screamed at me like I was on fire.

"I am not a baby."

"You're my baby."

And with that I picked her up and gave her a big hug. She hugged me back in her usual playful way. She might have just been playing, but that was one of the special moments in my life that I always looked forward to, her hugs. Needless to say, I loved her with all my heart.

"LET'S GO!!!"

"I'M COMING!!!"

I looked at my daughter. "What's wrong with your mother," I asked. Not really expecting an answer.

"You married her," was her reply.

"Not by choice, I was forced into it."

"Daddy, you know you love mommy," she said.

"You know I do, but just don't let her know it." She laughed and promised not to. She said that she would keep it a secret forever if I wanted her to. "That's my girl."

Emily finally walked down the stairs. She had her bags in hand and appeared to be ready for the day.

"Finally," I said.

"Well, good morning to you too," she replied with a grin as she leaned over to give me a good-morning kiss.

"Good morning," was my answer right before our lips touched. I wrapped my arms around her to pull her in close. I tried to savor the moment for as long as I could, before....

"YUCK!"

I knew that was coming. For someone to love to hug and kiss as much as Crystal did, she sure hated it when my wife and I showed affection.

"How do you think you got here?"

"Stop," Emily said right before she punched me in my arm. "She is only five. She does not need to here about stuff like that."

"I was joking. Come on baby, you know I was joking."

We finally were ready to get out of the door. Crystal put on her coat and Emily was finally finished putting on her face. I went around, turning all of the lights off. Everyone was ready and we headed out the door.

The car ride was the same as it was every other day. Crystal and I would laugh and tell jokes to each other while Emily would seemingly begin to stress about her upcoming day. Emily would laugh every now and then, but she mainly looked out of the window in an attempt to tune us out.

"Are you ready for work," I asked Emily. I knew that she hated her job, but we needed the money.

"Ready as I'll ever be."

I held her hand as we pulled up to the glass building. She looked at me like she was not ready for the day. I looked at her like if she didn't get out the car I was going to push her out.

"You know, it wouldn't hurt you to be a little sensitive. You know that I hate this job. You know that I hate going in here. So, why do you look at me like that every day?"

"Cause Emily, it is just work. All you are doing is typing up documents everyday for rich people who don't have the time. And everyday you sit here for like ten minutes just looking around like the building is going to change."

"I just don't want to go in, can't you understand that?"

"I do, but this is life. Sometimes life sucks. We just have to deal with it and make the best of it."

"I know, but it isn't easy."

She got out of the car. She opened the door to the back seat, leaned in and gave Crystal her customary kiss good-bye.

"Bye momma."

"Bye Crys."

"Bye baby."

"Bye Jim," she closed the door and started to walk towards the building.

"Let's go baby girl, time to get home."

We rush home, running late as usual and raced into the door.

"Shower, now," I said to Crystal as she dropped her coat on the floor. "Brush your teeth, wash your face and let's move."

"Yes Sir!"

I heard the water running in the bathroom. She went in and shut the door. Then the noise of the morning starts. *Bang! Bang! Bang!* There she goes again, beating the life out of the shower gel bottle trying to get the last drop out. I swear if it were a law against attacking soap, she would be doing life. *Bang! Bang! Bang!*

I ran into my room to get cleaned up for work. Not wanting to hear the all out assault on shower products, I turned my music on.

Bang! Bang! Bang!

I remember the first time I heard that commotion coming from the bathroom. I ran into the bathroom and tried to save the day like a superhero. Instead, I found a terrified four year old looking at me like I was going to kill her. When I found out what was going on, all I could do was laugh. From that day forward, I always left a half empty bottle in the shower. I believed that the attacking of the bottle gets her rage out for the day and I would prefer her to beat up on the bottle than one of her classmates.

"I'm ready," she screamed up the stairs.

"So am I," I screamed as I walked up behind her.

She jumped out of her skin. She then proceeded to attack me like that poor, defenseless bottle. She only came up to my stomach so her punches were pretty low. I am only thinking of protecting the sensitive area as she wailed away. She got in a couple of good stomach shots before I socked her in the arm.

"Ouch!"

"Well, stop playing then."

She put on the sad puppy-dog face and tried her hardest to make her eyes water up. I looked at her like I was truly sorry for hurting her then punched her in the other arm.

"OUCH!"

"Let's go woman!"

We raced to the car and headed off to her school. I dropped her off and she gave me my usual kiss on the cheek.

"I love you daddy."

"I love you too, baby."

She smiled and said, "I'm not a baby."

"You're my baby."

That night when I came home I found Crystal in the kitchen as usual. She was sitting at the table finishing up her homework. She loved homework. She loved to do her work while Emily finished work that she didn't finish during the day. Crystal would spell her words and count her pennies while Emily typed away on her laptop. As soon as I walked into the kitchen, Crystal jumped out of her chair and ran to me.

"Daddy," she said with excitement. "You're home."

"Yes ma'am I am. How was school?"

"Fun, Mrs. Thomason said I'm the best student in the whole kindergarten class. She said I'm the best speller and the best at math."

"That's wonderful. Is that homework finished? You have to keep that title, you know?"

"I'm almost finished. Can you help me?"

"Sure."

Emily looked up from her computer. "Hello Jim."

"Hello darling."

She hated when I called her that. She knew it was a fake response and that I didn't really talk like that.

"Whatever, I am going upstairs. I have to finish my work."

"Okay."

She grabbed her stuff and ran upstairs. This was how most of our nights were spent, Crystal and I downstairs doing something together while Emily was upstairs finishing work from the day. I guess I was used to it and that was why I was so close to her and she was so attached me to.

Right after Crystal was born, Emily came down with a terrible cold. Seeing as Emily was sick, she could not deal with Crystal because she didn't want Crystal to get sick. So, I took over all of the responsibilities of caring for Crystal. For the first couple of weeks, I took off work and spent morning and night caring for both of them. I would care for Crystal while she was awake and would try to nurse Emily back to health while Crystal slept. Eventually, I went back to work but nothing really changed. As soon as I would walk into the door, Crystal would be by my side and remain by my side until she fell asleep. I thought that was what good fathers did, so I welcomed it. It has been like that ever since.

Crystal grabbed about six books and ran over to me while I was looking into the refrigerator.

"Daddy, can I read you these?"

"Sure, let me grab something to eat first."

I grabbed a quick sandwich and headed for the couch. Crystal was already camped there with her first book cracked open and ready. I sat on the couch. Crystal crawled up under me and began to read.

"Little Chicken goes to.... goes to."

"School, sweetie."

She started again. "Little Chicken goes to School."

She read the book while I helped her with the big words. She is so intelligent. I sat there and listened to her read while I stare at her in amazement. She read the first three books and began to get tired. I picked up the last three books and read as she laid her head on my leg and drifted off.

Once I knew she was asleep I picked her up and took her to her bedroom. As soon as I went to lay her down she woke up and asked

12

that I stay in the room with her until she fell back asleep. Since this always happened, I pulled my blanket and pillow from under her bed and I laid out on the floor beside her. Just as she drifted off again, Emily came around the corner.

"Are you going to come to bed with me tonight?"

"Sure."

I got up and stuffed my blanket and pillow back under Crystal's bed. I gave her a kiss on her forehead and walked down the hallway and into my room. Emily was lying on the bed with her laptop resting on her legs.

"Did your wife let you out of her room?"

"Don't get smart," I said, tired of having the same conversation. "I can go back in there. I didn't come in here for all of this."

"Well, why did you come in here," Emily asked, as she moved her laptop to the side and sat all the way up. "What was your reason for coming in here?"

I knew what she was looking for. I knew that she wanted me to reassure her that I came in here because I loved her and wanted to spend time with her.

"I came in here for you."

"Whatever, you came in here because she is asleep. Your partner in crime crashed on you. That is the only reason why you are in here."

"Did you call me in the room for this? Just to fuss and argue. It is ten o'clock at night, I really don't have time for this."

With that, I left the room and walked back into Crystal's room. Crystal was still asleep. I grabbed my blanket and pillow and set up my bed up again.

Emily walked down the hallway and into Crystal's room.

"Jim. Jim, I know that you hear me."

"Can you please be quiet, Crystal is trying to sleep and so am I."

Emily walked back into the master bedroom and closed the door. I flipped my pillow and went to sleep, beside Crystal, like usual.

2

"Five minutes," I screamed up the stairs. I grabbed my coat and keys and headed towards the door.

"I'm coming," yelled Emily.

"I'm ready," Crystal said as she raced down the stairs. She jumped from the last step into my arms, and gave me one of the biggest hugs possible.

"Good morning daddy."

"Good morning sweetie," I said with a smile. "What in the world is your mother doing?"

"Putting on her face," was her answer. She grabbed her coat and went into the kitchen. She poured herself some juice in her favorite little, pink cup and walked back into the living room to sit down. There she sat, as she drank her juice and looked for something on TV.

"What are you doing?" I asked her. "Four year old girls can't pour juice."

"I'm five, daddy."

"You are?" I asked, like I didn't remember her birthday that just passed in December. She was born four days before Christmas.

She looked at me with pride in her eyes, like she had accomplished one of the greatest things that can be accomplished by a child.

"Yes sir I am."

Emily came down the stairs. Crystal and I simultaneously said, "Finally!"

Emily looked at Crystal with her evil mother look and said, "Excuse me." Then she looked at me with the same look, "You need to stop saying that. You know your little clone does everything you do. I wish you would think about things like that before you do and say the things that you do."

I looked around like I had no idea who she was talking to. "Are you talking to me?" Crystal laughed out loud; throwing more fuel on a fire that has started to burn inside Emily.

"Crystal," Emily shouted. "You need to be quiet. You do not laugh when adults are having a serious conversation."

"It was funny," I said as I interrupted her.

"I don't care. She should not be in adult conversations."

"Sorry mommy," Crystal said in the saddest voice possible.

"Let's go. We are running late."

I hated when Emily did that. I mean I would kick Crystal's butt when I needed to, but I would let the petty things go, and to me, that was very petty.

We left the house in a sour mood. The drive to drop Emily off made the mood worse, as there was no talking, no jokes and no laughter.

Once we dropped Emily off at work, I raced home as usual to get us ready for our day. We ran into the house and as usual I made the normal demand of, "shower, brush your teeth, and wash your face." But unlike normal, Crystal just walked over to the couch and sat down.

"Crystal, did you hear me? Crystal, don't make me hurt you, get up."

She got up slowly and dragged herself to the steps. She stood at the bottom of the stairs and just looked at me. I walked over to her, and with just enough strength to make her cry, pinched her butt. A tear rolled down her face as the pain set in. "Move it, we are late." She walked up the stairs as tears started streaming down her face.

Bang! Bang! Bang! Well, at least something is usual about this morning.

I walked upstairs, turned the music on and hopped in the shower.

Bang! Bang! Bang! Bang! Bang! Bang!

It was a war going on in that shower. The poor shower gel didn't stand a chance, not today. I wanted to go in there, but I figured that she had a terrible morning and she was blowing of steam. Again, I thought, (*better the bottle than some five years old face.*) Stomping sounds started coming from the shower, more banging sounds, and then nothing. I finished my shower, dried off and started to get dressed. The shower water was still running in the bathroom in the hallway. I threw on some shorts so I could see what was taking Crystal so long. I walked into the bathroom.

"Crystal sweetie, we have to go. Crystal?" No answer. I looked into the shower and she was gone. "Crystal," I yelled loud enough so that she could hear me from anywhere in the house. "Crystal! Where are you?" I walked around the house looking in every room. "Crystal!" I am starting to get upset. She ignored me once today and I let her off lightly, now she was ignoring me again. "Crystal, you better not be ignoring me. Crystal!" No answer. I am worried now. I ran to the front door, locked. I ran to the back door, locked. "Okay, she is in the house," I said to myself out loud. Maybe I just needed to say that to reassure myself that everything was okay. "CRYSTAL!" I know I said that loud enough for the whole neighborhood to hear me.

I walked to my neighbor's house. "Mrs. Smith, have you seen Crystal?"

"No, no I haven't," Mrs. Smith said, as she looked at me with concern in her eyes.

"I can't find her. She was in the house taking a shower and now she is gone."

"Have you called the police?"

"No, it just happened. I have been looking for her."

"You should call the police. Maybe they can help you look for her."

"Thank you."

I ran back to my house and dialed 911. I explained to the operator that my daughter was missing and I didn't know what happened. She said that she would get an officer out to my house as soon as possible.

An hour later a cop pulled into my driveway. By this time, I had gone completely crazy. The cop walked up and identified himself as Officer Mitchell with the Scottsdale Police Department.

"Well it's about time," I said with anger in my voice.

"Sir, calm down, I'm sure she is in the house, just hiding."

"Not this long, something is wrong."

"Sir, she could have just hid somewhere and fell asleep. It happens all the time. Did you have some sort of disagreement or falling out?" he said, as he sipped his cup of coffee.

"Officer Mitchell, my daughter is five years old. I don't have or would never have a 'falling out' with my five-year-old daughter. She does what I say and that's that."

"Sir, it is possible that she is hiding from you because she is afraid or angry. Let's search the house and…"

I jumped in before he could finish, "I ALREADY did that! She is not here! You have got to notify someone that she's missing. You have got to put out an alert or something. A five-year-old child just doesn't get up and walk away. DO SOMETHING!"

Officer Mitchell went back to his car and started talking to headquarters. After about two minutes he walked back up to me and stated that he needed to get a description of Crystal. He needed Crystal's height, weight, eye and hair color, last known outfit she might have been wearing, and names of anyone who might have wanted to take her.

"She is three feet, eleven inches, about fifty-five pounds, brown hair and brown eyes. She was in the shower, so I do not know what clothes she would have on." Instantly, tears rushed to my eyes. My five-year-old daughter, my baby, is out here in the world naked, being held by someone that could be doing anything to her. Anger hit me, and the first thing I thought was, *whoever did this must die.* Sadness hit me then because no matter what I could do to that person, I would never be able to take away what they might have done to her.

"The mother…. would the mother have taken the child?"

"No, she is at work." Then it hit me, I didn't tell Emily about the situation. I ran into the house and grabbed the phone.

"This is Emily Sutton, how may I help you?"

"Emily."

"What," she responded with the attitude that she had since last night and from the conversation this morning.

"Emily, you have to come home baby, Crystal is gone."

Instantly panic sets into her voice. "Gone, what do you mean gone? What happened? What did you do? Where did she go?"

"Emily," I jumped in. "You have to come home baby, I need your help. I have the police here now. Can you get a ride home?"

"I think so," her voice shaking. "I'm on my way."

Officer Mitchell was searching the house while I was on the phone with Emily.

"There are no signs of forced entry," he said as he was looking at the front door. He examined the panel, the door and the lock. He walked around the house looking at the windows, looking for any sign of someone breaking into the house.

Just then two more police cars pulled into the driveway. "Finally," I thought to myself, they are taking me seriously. The cops walked in and were briefed of the situation by Officer Mitchell. They walked outside to the backyard to see if they could find anything.

"Sir, would Crystal just get up and leave?"

"No, we taught her better than that. Crystal wouldn't even touch the door," I attested, remembering back to the one time I came down stairs on a Sunday morning and Crystal had gone outside by herself to get the newspaper. She scared the life out of me so bad when I didn't see her and the door was wide open. I beat her tail for that. She never touched the handle of the door since then.

Emily pulled up in a gray sedan. She jumped out and ran to the house.

"Jim," she called as she entered the house. She walked right up to me and hugged me with tears in her eyes. "What happened?"

"I don't know. All I know is that I was in the shower as usual. She was taking her shower. I finished and started to get dressed. Her shower was still going. I went into the bathroom to check to see what was going on and she was gone. I mean she just vanished into thin air."

Officer Mitchell jumped in. "Mr. and Mrs. Sutton, I am going to put out an Amber report for this child. This report is an emergency report that goes all across the U.S. It makes everyone aware that a young child has gone missing. Also, I am going to go talk to the neighbors. See if they have seen or heard anything."

"Thank you," Emily said. She turned to me, "Jim, what are we going to do? What are we going to do?"

"Just pray…. it's out of our hands."

That is all I wanted to say. That is all I could say. I could not let her know my real feelings. I could not fall apart; she was going to do that. When she came to the realization that this was for real, that this is not a "Lifetime movie", but it was real life, she would be no good to me. I had to stay strong for the both of us. I could not tell her that I was slowly dying inside. I could not drive around the neighborhood banging on everyone's door with a shot-gun demanding information. I had to say calm. I knew that I had to keep my thoughts straight if I ever wanted to get Crystal back. I could not let my brain play the 'what if' scenarios, it would drive me mad and then I would be no good and Crystal would be lost forever.

3

It has been two weeks now and still no word. I have officially lost my job, my happiness and my will to live. The police have found nothing and her face has long since stopped appearing on the TV. At first Emily and I clung to each other. After a couple of days, I could not deal with her, I could not really deal with anyone. She stayed at work all the time and would sneak into the house late at night, probably hoping that I would be asleep by the time she got home. When she realized that I couldn't sleep anymore, she stopped coming home all together. It has been a week since the last time I saw her. I called the police station everyday, and today was no different.

"Scottsdale Sheriff's Office."

"Good morning Maria." I had called so much we were on a first name basis. I knew that I was bugging the life out of her but she was the sweetest thing in the world. She never let on how much she wanted me to stop calling. Maybe she understood the pain that I was feeling and just wanted to be nice about it, or maybe she couldn't understand my pain and felt that I was entitled to call everyday, every minute if I wanted to. Either way, she answered the phone every time and never made me feel like a burden.

"Good morning Jim, are you hanging in there?" her voice sounding as gentle and caring as possible. I loved to hear her Spanish accent. It was the only thing that made me smile.

"Yes ma'am I am. Anything new today?"

"Let me check with Officer Mitchell. Hold please."

I hated this part. First, she puts me on hold with the worst hold music in the history of hold music. It sounds like someone more depressed than me playing a banjo. Then she comes back and tells me that they have not found anything and I will be the first to know when they do. She picks back up the phone and here we go again.

"Mr. Sutton," that is new, normally I am Jim. "Mr. Sutton, we need you to come in as soon as possible. How fast can you get here?"

"What is wrong? Did you find her? Is she alive? Oh goodness, you have to tell me what is going on."

"I can't. You have to come in as soon as possible. When can you get here?"

"Give me thirty minutes."

I hung up the phone. I immediately called Emily. Her answering machine picks up at work.

"Emily, this is Jim. I am going to the police station, they have told me to come in. I do not know if it is good news or bad news. Baby, please pray that they don't tell me bad news. Call me as soon as you get this or I will call you as soon as I know something. I love you, bye."

I hung up the phone and ran upstairs. I hopped in the shower to try to wash the dirt from the last two weeks off of me. I know I was dirty but being clean wasn't exactly a top priority. I took my time in the shower, mainly because I was scared to face what they might tell me. I could not take them looking at me saying that they found her body, I couldn't take it. What if they found her? I started to get excited with the thought that she might be waiting at the police station for me. That she would run up to me, hug me with one of her super hugs and just love me forever. I was filled with joy to think of her saying "Daddy." Then reality sets in. If they found her they would have brought her to the house. Shoot!!! That can't be it. They didn't find her. She can't be dead, she just can't.

I got out of the shower and raced to get dressed. I drove to the police station with millions of thoughts running through my mind and I was one squeeze away from using the bathroom on myself. I got to the police station and slowly walked through the door.

"May I help you sir?"

I knew that voice. It was Maria. "Yes ma'am, I am here to see Officer Mitchell. I called in earlier and was told to come to the station because they had some information on my missing daughter."

Instantly Maria knew who I was and why I was there. She told me to have a seat for a minute. She jumped up and walked into the back to get Officer Mitchell.

I looked around the police station. They had a big oak counter for when you walk in and talk to whatever officer was working the front desk. They had pictures of all the Most Wanted people pinned to the board sitting just above my head. It was just a basic police station, no more, no less.

Officer Mitchell walked out of the back. "Hey Mr. Sutton, how are you doing today?"

"I'm living." That is pretty much all I was doing. I was alive.

"Come on and follow me to the back. I just have a couple of things that I would like to go over."

I got up and followed him into a little room in the back. I sat down in the middle of the table; he walked to the other side of the table and sat directly in front of me. My stomach turned instantly. I was scared of what he might have to tell me. I just jumped right out.

"Did you find her?"

"We will get to that in due time."

"What do you mean "due time?" Did you find her?"

"Mr. Sutton, can you please go over what happened that morning?"

"I told you. We came home like always from dropping Emily off at work."

"And why did you drop her off at work?" he jumped in before I could finish telling him the story.

"Cause, we only have one car." I went on with the story as he wrote down some notes. "We came home, I went to take a shower and she went into the bathroom to take hers. I took my shower, finished, and started getting dressed. I noticed that her water was still running. I went into the bathroom to see what was going on and she was not there. I then ran around the house looking for her. I ran next door to ask the neighbor if she had seen her and then I called the police. I was looking for her until you got there."

He finished writing down everything that I was saying and left the room, stating that Detective Chambers needed to talk to me.

Mr. Chambers walked into the room. He was very tall, skinny, and didn't look happy at all. As soon as I saw his face, I instantly thought the worst. I thought he was going to tell me that she was dead, that they found her body in a trash can behind a fast food restaurant. I couldn't take it. I couldn't take him telling me that she was sexually abused until she died or until they killed her. My eyes watered up and tears started running down my face.

Mr. Chambers sat down. "Mr. Sutton, I just need to ask you a couple of questions."

"Is she dead? Please don't tell me she is dead."

"Well, you would know now wouldn't you?"

"What? What are you talking about?"

"Mr. Sutton, I went over the statement that you just gave to Officer Mitchell and I have a few questions of my own. First, what was all of the fighting in the house about?"

Fighting, what fighting is he talking about? I was confused by the question. "What?"

"Fighting sir, what was the fight about? We have statements from your neighbors that confirm there was a fight that morning in the house. Now, what was the fight about?"

"I have no idea what you are talking about. There was no fight. I told you I was in the shower and she was in her shower." Then it hit me. I know what they heard, the epic battle of the shower gel bottle versus the pissed off five year old, the battle that happened before she disappeared. Even if I explained the situation to him, he would never believe it. I was stuck.

"Sir, please answer the question, what was the fight about?"

"There was no fight. I was getting ready for work and she was getting ready for school just like every other morning."

"So, you fight every morning after you drop your wife off?"

"WHAT?" Before I can respond, he began his next question.

"Have you ever hit your daughter, Mr. Sutton?"

My body went numb. Of course, I have hit my daughter. She was my daughter. I had to spank her when she did bad things to teach her. I did not want her to grow up like these children that are bratty and disrespectful. I wanted her to know the difference between right and wrong. I wanted her to know that if she fell out in a store kicking and screaming because I wouldn't buy her something, I wasn't going to count to ten or pretend to leave her, but I was going to whip her butt.

I didn't know what to say because no matter what answer I gave, it wasn't going to be enough to get me out of this situation. I can't lie, so I told the truth. "Yes sir I have. I was her father and I disciplined her when the time called for it."

"You 'was' her father? Why are you talking about her like she is in the past? Is she in the past Mr. Sutton? Is she no longer here?"

"I don't know," tears really started to pour out of my eyes. "I assumed that you were or are going to tell me that she is dead."

"Mr. Sutton, you KNOW that she is dead."

"How do I know?"

"Why are you crying Mr. Sutton? Why don't you just tell me what really happened? Did you lose your temper that morning? You couldn't take it anymore? Did she mouth off at you and you thinking that you were going to teach her respect start to beat her? Did it go too far?"

I cried and shook my head no.

"Don't lie to me Mr. Sutton. We have witnesses that say you had a fight that morning. We have your neighbor that said you didn't even call the police until she suggested it."

"I was looking for her," I said, trying my hardest to talk clearly without my voice cracking. "I was looking for her!"

"You were the only one in the house. We know that you had the opportunity. We know that you had the means to do it. You are six feet tall and you weigh 245 pounds. She didn't stand a chance against you, did she?"

I am still shaking my head no. "I would never hurt her."

"Yes you would. I have statements that you have made to her in front of your neighbors. You told her you would beat the life out of her for crossing the street. Crossing the street deserves that kind of beating?"

My voice got low. I was trying to talk but I was feeling like someone had sucked all of the energy out of my body. "I said it to scare her. She just ran across the street without looking. She scared me to death."

"Did she scare you two weeks ago?"

"I loved her. I still do. She was my heart, my every thing."

"That wasn't my question."

I continued like I didn't even hear him or acknowledged his existence. "I would have done anything for her. I would have died for her. She was the reason my heart pumped blood. She was the reason I got up in the morning, the reason I woke up. She was my life."

"We found the body."

The words hit me like a ton of bricks. My head sank down into my chest. She is dead. She is dead. She is dead. I can't believe it. He looked at me waiting for my reaction. He was waiting for me to do or say something. I couldn't move. I was stuck. I knew it. I knew from the look on his face that they found her body, that she was dead. I knew it.

He threw pictures of a little girl that had been set on fire. Nothing remained of her, just a burnt up body laid out in what looked like a field. I shook my head in disbelief as I picked up one of the photos and look at it.

"No baby," I said as I started to run my fingers across the top of the head in the picture attempting to stroke her hair like I used to, "this can't be you."

"It's her. We have already matched the dental records and had it confirmed. It is Crystal, Mr. Sutton. Now, why did you do it?"

My sadness turned to anger. "You think I did this? Have you lost your mind? Is that what you sorry, no good, doughnut eating cops do here? You allow my child to get murdered when you are supposed to be out looking for her. Then, when you can't find her you wait for her to show up dead and then look for someone to blame? Is this what my taxes are paying for?" I picked up the pictures and threw them at him. Just then three police officers rushed into the room, guns drawn. "What do you want?" I shouted at them. "Did the doughnut light come on outside the door?"

"SIT DOWN," shouted Detective Chambers. He had enough of my ranting and raving but the only problem was that I was nowhere near finished.

The three officers left the room and Detective Chambers
started again with his interrogation. He asked question after question.
Repeatedly asking me what happened that day, what went wrong, and
what did I do. I repeatedly stated the exact same answer over and over
again.

"You know that we found fingerprints at the scene and I am
pretty sure once we get your fingerprints, they are going to match up.
We also found a hair, dark brown, just like your hair Mr. Sutton.

"Well, unless my daughter was killed at Dunkin Donuts, you
haven't found anything."

I guess six hours of questions and six hours of my replies was
more than enough for him. He ran around the table and jumped into
my face.

"Tell me you sorry excuse for a human, WHY did you kill
her?"

"I didn't kill her! How many times do you want me to say it?"

Six more hours of interrogation went on before they got the
okay to put me in jail. They had enough circumstantial evidence to not
allow me to walk out of the building. They charged me with the
kidnapping and murder of Crystal. They read me my rights and took
me to a holding cell. They asked me if I wanted to contact my lawyer.
I didn't have a lawyer. I didn't even have a job to pay for a half way
descent lawyer. They told me that they would arrange a meeting with
a court appointed attorney.

I can't believe it. I just can't believe it, my Crystal is dead and
worse, they think I did it.

4

"Why did you do it?" Scott, my public defender, asked as soon as he sat down. Immediately following his question I knew I was going to lose.

"I didn't do it!"

"I can see if they will accept a plea bargain. Manslaughter will only get you 15 years with good behavior."

"Why would I plea if I didn't do anything?"

"Mr. Sutton, this is a case that you can not win. I am your representative and I believe that you did it. How can I convince a jury that you are innocent when I can't even convince myself?"

"Well, maybe I need another lawyer. Maybe I need someone who believes me."

He lowered his head and removed his glasses. He looked at me struggling to keep a straight face. "No one believes you. No other lawyer at the office would touch this case. I took it to try to save you from yourself, to try to give you a way out and hopefully a future. If you go into that courtroom and claim innocent, they are going to put you away for life. Do you understand? You will go away for the rest of your life, no parole."

"I didn't do it. My daughter was murdered and no one is trying to do any kind of police work. No one is investigating anything. They are just trying to accuse me and shut the case."

There was a brief moment of silence. Then he spoke.

"Well, I think we have covered enough for today. They will take you to county lock up. I will meet with you soon to go over the case."

With that he grabbed his briefcase and headed for the door. The deputies came in to take me to the County Jail.

I went through the wonderful process of getting booked. I was fingerprinted, given the infamous mug shot and I gave my final statement to them. I was taken to Greens County Prison, fifty miles away from Scottsdale. I walked into this prison feeling like all I knew was just ripped away from me. I was scared because I heard all of the horror stories of prison. I was scared because of all the television shows that I saw regarding prison life. But mostly, I was scared because I knew going to jail for killing a five year old girl would make me an enemy of everyone in the prison, even though I didn't do it. I am sure that they have heard that before and me saying it would be no more believable than when the man before me said it.

I was one of ten new inmates to the prison. Every room we walked in, we heard the door slam behind us and we would have to stand there until the next door opened. I received my clothes, sheets and pillows for my bed and minor health care stuff like soap and a toothbrush. When I walked into population, where all the inmates and cells were, I felt like a spotlight was shining on me. One of the guys who came on the same bus started throwing things at some of the inmates in their cell. The inmates started going crazy as the guards rushed over and tackled the guy. Needless to say, the inmates were out to get him and he didn't make it through the night. They found him in the morning with his wrist cut. They probably would have suspected suicide if he wasn't tied to his bed. There was so much blood on the bed that it looked like a used maxi pad from a two hundred and fifty pound woman with thin blood.

With him out of the way, the spotlight turned back onto the rest of us. Everyday, everyone watched us. A few of the inmates would talk to me. They would tell me about what caused them to come to Greens and would always ask the same question, "Why are you here?"

Afraid of the ramifications of telling them, I would always respond with the same answer, "I didn't do it." They would laugh and say that no one here did it. Everyone here is innocent. To that I would respond that I was in the right place then. If this is where the innocent people go, then I must be at home.

A few weeks later my lawyer came to visit me. We met for a private conversation to go over my case.

"So, why did you do it," he said standing by the door. He was acting like he really didn't want to be there, like he had something of more importance to do.

"I told you, I didn't do it." I can't believe this is the guy that is supposed to be defending me. This guy is worthless.

"I can't help you unless you help me. Look, I am going to accept the plea. They will knock the charge down to manslaughter and this case will be closed."

"Look, this is my life. That was my daughter. If you don't want to follow through with the case, then quit. Get someone in here who actually wants to do their job and defend me."

After saying that, he banged on the door. "This conversation is over, I will see you in court." The officer came to the door and let him out. As Scott is walked out of the door, he whispered something into the officer's ear. The officer is looked at me smiling and nodding his head in approval while Scott whispered something to him. Scott finished his quiet conversation and walked off.

The guard walked over to me and stood me up to put the cuffs on me. As he was putting the cuffs on my wrist, he whispered in my ear, "You should have taken the deal."

"Are you my lawyer now?"

"What is about to happen to you, you are going to need more than a lawyer."

He walked me out of the room and down the hall to a small room where they do full body searches. They check every inch of your body and clothes to make sure your visitor didn't give you anything. Once they completed the search, he took me to the door that separated the hall from population. He shouted out, "Open door." As soon as the door opened, he started shouting, "Child murderer coming though!"

What, has he lost his mind? He is trying to get me killed.

"Child murderer coming through! He murdered a five years old girl and set her on fire."

I looked at him. "What are you doing?"

He kept shouting like he didn't even know I was there. "Child murderer boys!"

With that announcement, every inmate that was in his cell looked out to see who he was talking about. I felt like I was in a lion's den and they dressed me in a deer costume. Some started to yell and scream. Some pointed at me and started to tell me about all of the fun they planned to have with me. I didn't take the plea and my lawyer was upset about it, so upset that I didn't want to close the case, that he was going to have the prisoners close it for me.

5

Now there were different kinds of groups in Greens. You had your "White Supremacy" group, who thought everyone outside of the white race was below them. You had two groups of Muslims, one who hated everyone outside the black race and the one who taught peace and understanding. You had your homosexuals, some in the closet and some who had put pink bows and pom-poms on their closet. You had your Old Timers, the ones who have been in prison for the majority of their life. They mainly stayed to themselves and were respected by everyone in the prison. No one really bothered the old timers and if you did, you wouldn't survive in Greens too long. You had your drug dealers and drug users. You had your loners who walked around looking for a place to fit in. They were more like free agents and depending on the group, they were drafted, signed, or eliminated. It was like a jungle. One group was not going to let another group get so big that they could run the prison. So, if you were white and a free agent, if you didn't sign with the "White Supremacy" soon after your arrival, rival groups would eliminate you quickly. Even though you might never sign up with anyone, they didn't take the chance.

You had the "Untouchables". It was only one left in all of Greens. His name was Anthony, but everyone called him Tony. He was a six foot, five inches tall man that was 253 pounds of straight muscle. You didn't talk to him. You didn't look at him in the wrong way. You didn't even mention his name in a sentence. If you knew another Anthony or Tony and was telling someone a story about him, his name better had been changed to Tim. I witnessed the worst that Greens had to offer, quiver and shake when Tony walked passed. I have no idea what made him untouchable, but for him to have that kind of respect and fear from these kinds of people, it had to be something unthinkable.

Then there was my group, the "Dead Man Walking" group. You were considered in this group not because you were on death row, but because you have harmed a woman, child or someone of advanced age. If you raped, murdered, molested, kidnapped, tortured......... you get the point, you were the official enemy of everyone in Greens. The only way you could survive was by signing with a group quick in order to receive protection from everyone else. Without protection, a "Dead Man Walking" was a free target to any group that wanted to end his life. Every dead man walking was given a number level of how bad you had to die, one, being that you had to die within the three months of your arrival at Greens, ten, being that you could not make it through the night.

Unfortunately for me, I never wanted to get involved with all of that. When I first arrived here, I was not trying to get mixed up with all of the groups and gangs. Once word got out about why I was here, I was given a level nine. I was supposed to be dead by the end of the week and the day was Thursday.

Everyone started gunning for the level nine. That night, in my cell, my cellmate wrapped his sheet around my neck and started choking me. He was only five feet tall and about 150 pounds but he was strong. I pushed him into the cell bars as he struggled to keep the sheet tight around my neck.

When the other inmates heard the commotion, they started cheering for him to finish the job. They shouted, "Kill that nine! Kill him!"

The guards ran up to my cell door and watched as he tried to kill me. We struggled for about two minutes until I was able to overpower him and get the sheet from around my neck. I pushed him into the toilet as I dropped to the ground and gasped for air. Just then the guards rushed into the cell and proceeded to club me repeatedly; bashing me over my head and jamming the club into my ribs. They removed me from the cell and put me in another cell for the night. The prisoner in this cell was an Old Timer. Even if he wanted to kill me, I don't think he had the strength or energy to follow through with it. They didn't want to throw me in the hole or take me to the prison's infirmary because they wanted the job finished as soon as possible.

The next day while taking a shower, I felt a sharp object enter into my side. I looked down to see my flesh getting ripped open by a blade. I pushed the man back and he fell into a group of "White Supremacy" members. He was one, or at least a loner trying to get into the group. Just then, I felt another object penetrate the back of my shoulder. I swung around to see a member of the Muslims group with blood all over his hands. They were going to kill me, right there, right then.

I started to scream for help, but no one came. I started to fight back. I punched the "White Supremacy" guy as he ran back over to attack me. I hit him around his cheek, crushing his jawbone. He fell to the ground, dropping his knife in the process. I then turned my attention to the member of the "Muslim" group. He launched himself at me with the knife in his right hand, trying to go for my throat. I grabbed his hand and struggled with him, trying to get him to drop his knife. Another member of the "Supremacy" picked up the knife that fell from the first guy and tried to stab me. As he attempted to attack me, the struggle that was going on with the other guy resulted in us spinning out of control and he got stabbed in the back of his neck. Then a war broke out in the shower. The "Blacks" attacked the "Whites" and everything went back to the way it used to be; the way it was before I became a Nine and the target of everyone.

The guards rushed in and broke up the fight. At the end of it, six people got stabbed and sent to the prison infirmary. I was one of the six. The first guy who stabbed me died from three stab wounds to the chest. So did the second guy, the black guy, he died from the stab wound to the neck. I, on the other hand, was stabbed seven times, all over, received over 75 stitches and was rushed back into population in a week. The other three survivors stayed in the infirmary for a month and they had minor stuff compared to me.

The first day out of the infirmary, Scott arranged for an emergency meeting. He walked into the room, sat down on the other side of the table and put his briefcase in front of him. He opened his briefcase and pulled out some papers.

"Mr. Sutton, I have the plea, just sign right here and all of this will be over with," he said, pointing to an X on the paper with his pen. "You do not want this to go on. Look at you. You are bleeding through your jumpsuit." He pointed down to my stomach to show me where blood had started to bleed through my shirt. "Come on, let's close this so that we can both move on with our lives."

"So, if I sign this paper, all of this goes away."

"Sure, if that's what you want to happen, then yes, it goes away."

"And I get Crystal back, she comes back to life. I get to go home, get my job back and none of this ever happened, right?"

"Well, no…"

I jumped in before he could even finish his thought. "Then how are you telling me that we can both get on with our lives? How is this paper going to do anything for me? You get to go back to your life, my life is over regardless."

"But you have a life and this paper will ensure that you keep it."

"How? Are you going to call the dogs off? Did you really think that you could open up that box and close it when you get good and ready? They are going to try to kill me regardless of whether or not I sign that paper. As a matter of fact, if I did sign that paper and confessed, they would really come after me." I know that they were attacking me already, but I knew that there were some people on the fence; some people who the verdict was still out on. I couldn't make the verdict for them. I had to keep as many people at bay as possible.

"Here is a wild and crazy idea, and I know I am going out on a limb here, but how about we talk about the case and my defense. You know, maybe go over what you are going to say in court. I mean that is what I thought lawyers do," I said sarcastically.

"I have taken care of the defense, you do not need to worry about that."

"Yeah, well what are you going to say? What is our defense?"

"I just said don't worry about that," and with that he grabbed his papers, threw them back into his briefcase and got up to leave. He banged on the door to be released from the room. "I will see you in court in two weeks."

"Great. See you then."

6

It was the day before my first court appearance. The last two weeks have been pretty much the same. At first, I would get attacked by someone or get stabbed by someone, I would fight back, and get attacked by more people. It just got to the point where I stopped fighting. If someone were to hit me, I would take it and walk away. If someone were to jab me with a knife, I would cover the wound and run for help. The more I fought, the more that would come. No matter how much I fought I could never get the upper hand. It was just too many of them that wanted to take me out.

That night I was lying in my cell thinking about the big day. I was going over what I was going to say and what I wanted to say. I wanted to get the truth out. I wanted to let everyone know how much I loved Crystal and would do anything for her. I wanted them to feel the love that I had for her, the love that I still have for her.

My cellmate, the "Old Timer," kept tossing and turning in his bed. He was restless. Normally as soon as they called for lights out, he would be sleep within five minutes. It was at least four hours past that time and he wasn't asleep yet. Something was wrong.

Just then, my cell door opened. As soon as he heard the door, he jumped out of bed and went under it. Five men ran in and pulled me off of the top bunk, slamming me to the hard concrete floor. They proceeded to stomp on me, punch me and beat me with some kind of wooden object. I tried to crawl under the bed, but the "Old Timer" kept pushing me back out while the men grabbed me to stop me from getting away. I don't know how they all fit in my eight by five cell, but they did. They repeatedly kicked me and repeatedly clubbed me. I didn't fight back. I just covered my face and curled up in a ball.

After several minutes of punishment, the men left the cell and the door closed. I lay on the ground bleeding and shaking. The "Old Timer," everyone called him Uncle Don, crawled from under the bed. He pushed me against the back wall by the toilet and proceeded to pee on me. Once he was done, he spat on me, called me a piece of trash and climbed back into his bed and went to sleep. I just lay there. I couldn't move.

The next morning the guards came to get me for court. They walked into the cell and kicked me in my back to wake me up. They dragged me to the shower, turned the water on and threw me in there. I just let the water run down my face. It burned like fire because of all the cuts and bruises. I didn't even attempt to wash myself. I just stood there, bleeding and in pain.

After the shower they took me to a holding cell where I was to wait for my attorney. Scott walked in and immediately called for the guards. The guards rushed to the room.

"Guards, take this man to the infirmary. He is in no shape to go to court today."

The guards walked over to pick me up.

"No, I am fine. Leave me alone."

"Mr. Sutton, you have to go to the infirmary. You need medical attention as soon as possible."

"I am fine. I can make it."

"I won't hear of it. Guards, take him to the infirmary."

The guards grabbed me by my arms and dragged me out of the room. At first, I felt kind of at ease that someone actually cared that I just got the life beat out of me. But then it hit me, Scott never cared about me or what was happening to me. As a matter of fact, he was the one who started the whole thing. I planted my feet and started to resist.

"No, I am going to court." The guards grabbed me and started to pull me down the hallway. "No, I have to go to court," I screamed as they tried to restrain me. I was yelling so loud that I was drawing the attention of everyone in the courthouse. They had no choice at that point, they had to let me go to court.

Scott was sitting at the defense table when they brought me in the room. A couple of reporters were in the courtroom taking pictures. They had an artist in the room drawing me as I walked in. They took the cuffs off me and allowed me to sit next to Scott.

He leaned over, "Listen, just allow me to do all of the talking. The judge is going to ask you a couple of questions and all you have to do is say yes. That is all."

That seemed simple enough. Just say yes a couple of times and I was out of there. Only problem was that I didn't trust Scott. He didn't want me there that day, for some reason or another. I had to find out why.

Judge Johnson started talking, "In the case of State versus Mr. Sutton, Mr. Sutton, how do you plea." Scott stood up and responded, "Honorable Judge Johnson, the State and Mr. Sutton have reached a plea bargain. You have been given all of the information along with the signature of Mr. Sutton agreeing to accept the plea."

I looked at Scott like I could have killed him. He set me up. He set all of this up. He had them beat me last night so that I wouldn't be able to come to court today. That is why he was so bent on me going to the infirmary.

The judge looked at me. "Mr. Sutton, have you agreed to the terms and conditions of this plea bargain?"

"No, your honor." The State's Attorney looked at Scott. Scott turned blood red in the face and looked at me.

"I told you to say yes to everything."

I continued to talk to the Judge like I didn't even hear what he was saying. "No your honor. I have not agreed to anything and if you have any kind of paper with a signature on it, it is not mine."

With that, panic set in on Scott. He didn't know what to do. I wasn't supposed to be here. I was supposed to be in a comma or something. I was to be in the infirmary lying on a bed getting examined.

Scott jumped up, "Your Honor, I request a thirty minute recess to speak with my client, please."

"It appears that you have a lot to talk about counsel. You have one hour to clear up this confusion and when you come back, I expect to hear that he is either taking the plea bargain or he is ready to enter a plea of guilty or not guilty. Do you understand?"

"Yes, Your Honor."

The Judge dismissed the courtroom for one hour. Scott grabbed his briefcase and stormed out of the courtroom as the deputy put the handcuffs back on me. He took me to a small room in the courthouse where Scott was waiting for me. The deputy took me in the room, sat me down, and left the room to stand guard outside the door.

Scott walked up to me and said, "What do you think you are doing? I told you to say yes to whatever questions he may ask. All you had to do was say yes and all of this would have been over with. What do you think, that you can win? You can't win. I know that you can't win. I have been a lawyer for twenty-five years and I have seen winners and losers and believe me Jim, you are a loser."

"Then quit. Why are you even wasting your time and mine?"

"Because this is my job and I have to defend you."

"Then start doing your job and defend me. Have you even tried to think of how to defend me in this case? Have you asked me about anything that happened? Have you asked me my side of the story? The only thing that you are worried about is getting a deal done so you can go back to your life. I told you before, if I quit, this just doesn't disappear for me. If I take a deal, I am a dead man for sure."

Scott looked at me, "If you don't deal, do you think that you are going to live?"

7

"All rise, court is now in session," the bailiff shouted across the courtroom. We stood up as the judge walked into the room, looked around and then took his seat. As the judge sat down, so did everyone else.

"Mr. Sutton, it is under my understanding that you are not taking a deal that was worked out between your lawyer and the Prosecution."

I stood back up, "That is correct, your honor."

"Do you understand that if we continue with this and go to trial I will not accept any plea bargain? Once we start this, we will go all the way to the end. We will reach a verdict."

"I understand your honor."

"Prosecution, you may proceed with your opening statement."

With that my downfall began. The State's Attorney started with his opening argument. He told them about how she died. How someone kidnapped her. How someone choked her. How she was barely alive, but still alive, when she was set on fire. He drilled the point home with the jury about how I was the only one in the house and the only one with the opportunity to murder Crystal. I was the last person to have seen her alive. There were no signs of forced entry into the house. No doors appeared to be tampered with and no windows were broken. There was no one else that was in the house because Emily, Crystal's mother, was at work at the time. No one else lived in the house. No one else had a key to the house.

He then pointed to me and repeatedly said, "Mr. Sutton killed Crystal. He killed her. He killed her, and we are going to prove it."

He sat down and Scott got up. Scott walked over to the jury and stared directly at them. "Ladies and gentlemen, my client is innocent."

He then turned around and walked back towards me. He sat down and started to write something on his notepad.

"Is that it?" I whispered to him.

"Yup. No more to say than that."

I just shook my head as the judge ordered the prosecution to call their first witness. He called Officer Mitchell. He asked about all the information he found at the house. He asked about my state of mind when he arrived. He asked about any information that was given to him by the neighbors. He finished his line of questions and Scott got up to cross- examine the witness. Scott again asked about my state of mind and asked him if he felt like I was upset because I lost my child or upset because I just murdered her. Mitchell stated that he couldn't tell. Scott asked about the fight in the house and whether or not that had something to do with my state of mind. Mitchell stated that the fight could have had a lot to do with my state of mind.

Game over.

It hit me at that point that there were two prosecutors and no one to represent the defense. He talked about the fight even though the prosecution had not brought it up. He tried to get the point across to the jury that something bad happened in the house and I did it. He was going to make sure I was convicted of this.

The prosecution called witness after witness and they all testified to pretty much the same thing, I was the only one in the house and Crystal is dead. Beyond that, the State really didn't have much else. My only problem was my attorney was playing prosecution assistant and wanted me to get guilty more than anyone in the courtroom. My trial lasted for two days. The prosecution had called all of their witnesses on the first day. The second day the State rested. Scott didn't have any witnesses to call so the Defense rested also. The jury was deliberating for all of twenty minutes before they reached a verdict of guilty of murder in the first degree.

My sentencing was done after the verdict was read. The judge talked about the malice of the murder. How he was sickened with the fact that a father could do that to his daughter. How he couldn't imagine the feeling she must have felt to see her own father choking her. He said I left him no choice but to give me life without the possibility of parole. He said the only reason he was not giving me the death penalty was because the prosecution didn't ask for it.

I smiled and said to myself, "Don't worry, Greens will take care of that for you."

Once word of my trial reached Greens everyone on the fence jumped off. I venture to say that about one fourth of the prison's population was out to get me. The rest of the seventy five percent was either too old, was trying to survive themselves, or just didn't care about what was going on.

Everything became three times as difficult. I was already having a hard time as it was. I got punched, kicked or stabbed daily. Everyone wanted to step to me, even the little nobodies. I had punks, prison girls, that ran up to me and slapped me my face. I couldn't do anything. I couldn't fight back because as soon as I looked like I was going to throw a punch, twenty people would surround me. So I ran, and I kept running.

In the courtyard, I just tried to remain invisible. I would find the corner of a fence or go to the corner of the building and sit. I figured if I had the building behind me, all I had to do was to watch my front side and look out for attacks. At first it worked for a while, until some guys figured that I was already cornered so I couldn't run. They would walk up and surround me while two or three of them watched out for the guards. I really don't know what they watched for, the tower guards didn't care if they killed me. They would beat me and beat me until they got tired or some other guards would run over and break it up.

Eating became impossible. Every time I went to get food, someone would spit in it or blow their nose in it. Once I could no longer take the hunger pains, I tried to eat around the stuff they would put in my food. That didn't last too long because they started to cover the whole plate. Sometimes I would get my tray and it would smell like urine. Prison life was hard by itself, but they made it suicidal.

8

Two years has passed since my trial took place and I have been in and out of the infirmary during the entire two years. Normally I would go for stab wounds or bruises all over my body that I suffered from nightly attacks. They would sew me up or patch me up as fast as possible and have me back into population in a day or two. Some guys would twist an ankle and get a week in the bed. I nearly bled to death one morning and they had me back into my cell that night. I think the more I came in there, the more they got upset that I wasn't dead. After two years of this, I was starting to get upset myself. I mean just finish the job.

One day, as we were about to get released from our cells for exercise, a guard came and knocked on my cell bar.

"You have a visitor."

Was he talking to me? He was looking at me, but who in the world would come to visit me? I hadn't heard from Emily in over two and a half years. I don't even know if she knew I was in here. My parents passed away long ago. I didn't have family that I kept contact with.

I got up and walked to the door. He handcuffed me through the bars and took me to a small room. He took the handcuffs off and told me to sit down. He walked out and soon after a woman walked in. She was wearing a blue business suit and I could see her badge and gun hanging off her belt. She sat down on the opposite side of the table directly in front of me.

"Mr. Sutton, my name is Detective Diaz from the Scottsdale Police Department. I just have a couple of questions for you."

She pulled out a big brown envelope and handed it to me. I opened the envelope and pulled out a stack of about ten pictures. I flipped the pictures over and looked at them. It was Crystal. It's a picture of Crystal on the swing when she was four years old. I sat there looking at the picture as a tears rolled down my cheek.

"Why did you do it, Mr. Sutton? Why did you kill that little girl?"

I just sat there looking at the picture. I finally looked up at her. "You got your guilty verdict. I am in here for life. What else do you people want from me?"

"I want to know why you killed her. What possessed you to do that…" she paused, trying to hold back the tears. "What would possess you to hurt a beautiful little girl like that?"

"I didn't," I said looking back down at the picture of her on the swing.

"Mr. Sutton, you are going to have to do better than that. That is all you are saying but you have no proof that you didn't do it."

"Mrs. Diaz, I thought in this country you were innocent until proven guilty. I don't have to prove that I didn't kill Crystal, you have to prove that I did."

"Well we did that Mr. Sutton. Thank you for your time." She reached for the photos that were in the envelope.

"Why did you come here, Maria?"

"It is Detective Diaz. I came here because I had to ask you myself. You called me everyday about that little girl and I just wanted to know what kind of sick animal would do that when he knew what he had did. I see now. I see what kind of person you are."

"And what kind of person is that?"

"A dirty no good dog, a person that deserves to be beaten everyday like they have beaten you. You don't deserve to see the light of day. I was hoping that they would have killed you by now. I hate you Jim. I hate you for making me feel sorry for you. I hate you for making me care about Crystal and look for Crystal when you knew she was dead."

Tears rolled down her face as she got up to leave. Before she could bang on the door, I called to her.

"Maria, sorry, Detective Diaz, you want proof that I didn't kill Crystal?"

She stopped and turned around. "I'm listening," she said wiping her face with a tissue as she tried to compose herself. She walked back to the table and sat down.

"When Crystal was born I was all she had. Emily was sick and she could not take care of her, so I had to."

"What does this have to do with anything?" she shouted at me with anger. "This has nothing to do with what happened!"

"Detective Diaz, you asked for proof, this is my proof. Can I please finish?"

She nodded her head and I continued with the story.

"Crystal and I have been together since birth. I was the first person she had seen in her life. I was the voice that sang to her at night to put her to sleep. I fed her, bathed her, and clothed her more times than everyone else in this world combined. I breathed for her and she breathed for me. She was everything to me. She was the reason why I lived."

Maria put her head down. "Jim, that still doesn't explain what happened to Crystal. Okay, you loved her and she loved you. I have seen what people do to the ones they so called love. I have a file door full of crimes that have been committed by loved ones. That is not proof."

"When Crystal was around eighteen months she began to realize that I would leave for work everyday. She would wake up every morning and crawl down the stairs and run to the front door. She would stand in front of the door so that I couldn't leave. When I would pick her up, give her a kiss, and hand her to Emily, she would cry. She would cry and yell for me as I walked down the sidewalk and get into the car. It ripped me up inside. The first couple of times it happened I didn't go to work. I called out sick and stayed home with her. Eventually, I got enough heart to drive off while she was crying. I felt like the worst father in the world. I felt like I was lower than the lowest creature on this earth. Detective, I couldn't imagine my life without Crystal and what you are accusing me of is suicide, because for me to kill her would be like me killing myself."

Maria looked at me and for the first time in over two years, someone had felt sympathy for me.

"Jim, I can see that you loved her. From all that you told me, I get that, but that doesn't prove anything. That just doesn't prove that you didn't kill her."

"Detective, like I said at first, I shouldn't have to prove that I didn't kill her, you should have to prove that I did."

"And like I said, the State did."

There is a brief moment of silence as we both search for words to say to each other. I am still looking at the pictures, tears falling down my face, as I go from one to the other. I flip through all of the pictures and then look up at her.

"Well, I would like to thank you so much for being there for me during that time. I know that I was a pain in the butt. I really didn't mean to call you that much and bother you, but I was just looking for answers and I was hoping that you would have some."

"Please don't bring that up and please don't thank me for that."

"Why, I am being serious. I really want to thank you for not blowing me off or acting like I was becoming a burden."

"Why are you doing this? Why are you acting like you are this innocent man who did no wrong?"

"I am innocent."

"Yes Mr. Sutton, that is why you are in jail, because you are innocent. I am sure that everyone behind bars in this prison is innocent."

Maria jumped up again and grabbed the pictures. I pushed my chair back to try to avoid her hand.

"Mr. Sutton, please give me those photos. They are a part of the investigation that was done."

"Where did you get these from?" I asked flipping through them again.

"They were confiscated during the search of your house. We took a lot of things from your home."

"Can I keep these, please?"

"No you may not, those are considered evidence."

"Maria, I am begging you. This is my baby. Please, from one friend to another, please."

Just then I felt my stitches pop open. I was stabbed two days ago on the right side of my chest and the hole was not closed well enough. I felt the blood starting to seep through my shirt. Maria looked at me in horror as she noticed the blood coming through my shirt.

"What happened?" she shouted at me. She got up to bang on the door to get the guard.

"Just a little stab wound, I am okay, really," I said as I put my hand over the wound to try to stop the bleeding.

The guard rushed into the room to see what was going on.

Maria shouted at him to go get help. The guard ran and called for the medical team to come to the room. A doctor and two nurses rushed to the room as the whole right side of my shirt turned blood red. They took a towel and applied pressure to the wound as they rushed me to the prison infirmary. Once there, they sew me up again, this time stitching it twice so that it would hold.

A day later, I was back in my cell. When I arrived at my cell there was a package there waiting for me. It was a letter from Maria. It read:

Dear Jim,

I am going against my better judgment, but here. Please do not lose it because this is the only one you will receive. Take care of yourself.

Maria

I looked inside the envelope and there was a photo of Crystal eating spaghetti. Written on the back of it was:

The first time she said Daddy – 11 months old

9

I carried Crystal with me everywhere. Even though I was still in prison, looking at her picture made me feel almost human again. I kept it on me, under my shirt or in my pocket and pulled it out every now and then just to make me smile. I would get lost in thought looking at her. She made the days go faster and the nights more peaceful. Even though she was dead, and even though it was just a picture, I felt like a piece of my heart had been returned.

Walking through the courtyard of Greens looking at peace caught the eye of a lot of people. Some people thought I turned gay and was happy because I just finished getting plugged. Some thought I finally turned to drugs and was walking around high. Either way, they didn't like my newfound happiness and was determined to put an end to it.

That night, my cell door opening woke me up. I jumped up because I knew what was coming. Three guys rushed in and pulled me to the ground. I covered up and tried to slide under the bed. Two of them just grabbed me and held me down. The other one started searching my bed and looking into my pillow. Once he didn't find anything on my top bunk, he pulled the "Old Timer" out of his bed and started to search his. He still didn't find what he was looking for. Finally, he looked down at me on the ground.

"Where is the picture?" he said as he put his foot on my chest.

"What picture?"

One of the guys holding me down hit me in my mouth.

"Last time, where is the picture?"

I couldn't give my picture up. That is all I had. That gave me a fraction of my heart back and I couldn't lose it. I closed my eyes and braced myself for what was going to come.

"What picture?"

With that, the beating started. He kicked and punched me while the other two guys held me down. He ripped off my shirt to check to see if I had it hidden. He then started to check my pockets.

"NO!"

"No what, is it in here?" he asked as he went into my left pocket. He pulled out the folded up picture of Crystal. He opened it and just stared at it for a minute. He flipped it over and read the back. After he read it, he bent down to me and said, "Don't ever lie to me again."

"I didn't lie," I said as blood was falling from my mouth onto the ground. I didn't lie. I asked what picture, I never said that I didn't have a picture.

He looked back down at the picture, "Cute kid." He got up and started to walk out. The other two guys released me and got up to leave.

"No, please don't take my picture. That is all I got." I attempted to get up but my body was too weak.

He laughed at me and walked out of the cell. As soon as the other two men walked out the cell door closed.

I crawled to the door and screamed. "Please don't take it! Please don't take it! That is my little girl! Bring it back! Bring it back!" I couldn't contain myself. Tears streamed down my face and I screamed louder. "Please, just bring it back! BRING IT BACK!"

With all of my noise everyone started to wake up. Most of the prisoners screamed for me to shut-up. A few of them mocked me. Faking like they were crying and screaming, "Bring it back, bring it back!"

Uncle Don got up off the floor and got back into his bed. I was too tired and too weak to move, so I just sat there. I was hoping that they would bring the picture back but I knew that it was gone. I just sat there the rest of the night, tears steadily rolling, defeated.

I woke up the next morning from the sound of the cell door opening. It was time for roll call and then time to go to breakfast. Once they made sure that everyone was present and accounted for, they moved us out and headed everyone to the cafeteria.

I didn't eat breakfast. One reason was the spit all over my food but even if the food was edible, I just didn't feel like eating. I felt lost all over again. I felt like they just took the last piece of life away from me. The picture made me care again and they just stole that away from me.

After breakfast, we went back to our cell for a few hours. After that, we went to the courtyard for exercise. I went to my normal corner of the building. I learned the location of the guards who actually cared, so I made my spot right beside them. I still had the people who didn't care about the guards and would run up and attack me anyway. I would just cover up to protect myself until the guards pulled them off me.

Inmates who had been at Greens for a while wouldn't mess with me while I was standing next to the guards. They would usually talk to some new recruits or wannabes and tell them to attack me to prove their worth. They would do it despite the present of the guards, and the guards would beat them for doing it while they were standing there. Other guards wouldn't care, but I guess these particular ones took it as a sign of disrespect.

Today was no different. Some fools ran up and started to swing at me wildly. I balled up to protect myself as the guards ran over and started beating them with their wooden sticks. It wasn't a nightstick. It was much, much, thicker and hurt a whole lot more. The prisoners called it "pole control", because when they hit you with it, the guards took control and you lost all of it.

The guards took the men and sent them to the hole for a week. One of the guards asked if I was okay.

"I'm fine," I replied, dusting myself off. "Thank you for helping me."

"It wasn't for you. I have never had an inmate die under my watch and I am not about to let it happen now. If they want to kill you, they better do it on my day off."

The guard walked back over to the middle of the wall and proceeded to watch over the inmates. He stood there with the "pole control" in hand, waiting for the next fool to run up and take a shot at me. I think he liked it when I got attacked. Not because he wanted to see me hurt or killed, but because he like to beat the crap out of everyone dumb enough to do it in front of him.

I on the other hand, had officially had enough. I had taken their beatings. I had taken the stabs and the cuts. I had taken getting beaten in the middle of the night. I had taken everything they threw at me, but they took my picture. They took it and they were happy that they took it. They were satisfied that I was back to being miserable. They found joy in the fact that my life had hit rock bottom, again.

Imagine if you would, a cup. A tall, wide cup like the kings used to drink out of back in the medieval times. Now picture someone coming to pour a liquid into this cup. Juice, water, soda, it really doesn't matter, just some form of liquid. They start to pour the liquid and the cup gets full. Well, my cup was fixed. At first, my cup had a hole in it and everything that was poured into the cup went right out of it. Then a patch came to fix the hole when they took the picture of Crystal and now my cup can hold liquid, which to me, is anger. The more they poured, the more anger I felt.

That attack on me just gave me a nice quarter of a cup of anger. When I walked around the courtyard and back inside, every laugh, every joke, every comment just filled my cup up even more. When I went to lunch and they spit in my food, more liquid was poured into the cup. When we had free time around the prison and a queen ran up to me and smacked me, more liquid into the cup.

By the time dinner rolled around, the cup was pretty much topped off. I walked into the cafeteria and got my food, spaghetti with meat sauce. They added their normal flavoring to it.

I sat down at the table to try to pick through what they put in it. Spit was everywhere. I couldn't take it, not today. I put my spoon down in frustration and just sat there. I looked up and noticed a small group of men looking at me, laughing. One of the guys, people called him Chuck, picked up a hand full of spaghetti, smeared it all over his face, looked at me smiling and said, "Daddy."

All of the guys around him busted out laughing. He just kept repeating himself over and over again as they fell out laughing around him.

My cup was already full and I was already on edge. This guy had no idea what he just did. He just poured a gallon of milk into a shot glass.

I got up and walked past the table where they were sitting. Chuck was sitting at the end of the table. As I was walking past, he kept yelling, "Daddy! Daddy," and proceeded to laugh it up with his fellow inmates. I walked past him and headed towards the place where the trays were dropped off. When I noticed that they had stopped paying attention to me, I turned around and walked back towards their table. I picked up my pace as I approached the table.

Chuck had just finished wiping off his face and started to eat again. As soon as he put his spoon in his mouth, a tray hit him in the face causing the spoon to jam in the back of his throat. A tray had hit him. My tray had hit him. All of the other inmates at the table jumped back in shock. Chuck was pulling at the spoon, trying to get it out of the back of his throat. He probably would have been able to get it out if I didn't hit him again and again and again. I hit him until the guards rushed over and pulled me back.

Blood rushed out of his mouth. At first, it looked like spaghetti sauce, but it just kept flowing and flowing. Blood was everywhere and the guards tried to get him up and take him to the prison's infirmary.

Most of the guards were trying to get him up and out of the cafeteria while two of the guards were trying to restrain me. Needless to say, those two 160 pound guards didn't stand a chance against me.

I was able to break free as I rushed over to attack the other inmates that were laughing. Other guards had rushed into the cafeteria and cleared everyone out. We were going into lockdown, and I was going into the hole.

I rushed over and grabbed the only one I could get my hands on. I proceeded to choke him from behind as the guards that tried to restrain me at first, rushed over to get me. We all fell to the ground as they tried to break us up. They hit me, kicked me, pulled me and smacked me repeatedly with pole control, but I wouldn't let go. Finally, one of the guards ran over and shot me with a beanbag right into my ribs. As angry as I was, that sucked all of the life out of me. It felt like I was in a car accident. Like I had hit a tree going a hundred miles an hour and the steering wheel crashed into my ribs.

I let go. Not my choice but out of pain. I don't know if it was a good thing or a bad thing but they shot me too late. He was dead. I don't know whether it was from the lack of oxygen or from his neck getting broke from all of the commotion. Either way, he was not coming back anymore. He was paroled, permanently. Chuck died too, while lying in the cafeteria. He bled to death right there on the floor. There was nothing anyone could do.

They handcuffed me and took me to the hole. As they walked me from the cafeteria to solitary confinement, we had to pass through population. As we walked through, I started to shout, "Two down, a whole lot more to go."

The guards punched me to silence me, but they couldn't. I kept yelling. As we passed the halfway point, I felt a sting and burning pain on the right side of my neck. The guards rushed me out of there and took me to the infirmary. I didn't know what was happening until I saw the doctor pull a blade from my neck. Blood was running everywhere on the infirmary bed. I lost so much blood I blacked out. I thought I was dead. I thought they had finally finished me off for good, but that was okay. If I was going to die today, I wasn't going alone. I'd taken two with me, and that was good enough.

10

Two days passed before I came to. I was lying in an infirmary bed, neck bandaged up tightly. I found out that I was stabbed in the neck by a shank that an inmate threw. I guess it was from someone who was pissed about Chuck. Oh well, two down, a whole lot more to go.

I lay in the bed trying not to show everyone that I was awake. I knew that if they knew I was awake, I would be out of there by the end of the day. I glanced around the room looking for a nurse or a guard, but I didn't see any of them. I looked around the room for a minute and then closed my eyes again. I was going to take advantage this time. I wanted to get all the rest I could before I was thrown back into population.

Right beside me I heard the sound of what I thought was a man crying. Crying in Greens, that was a death sentence, even I knew that. He sounded like he was in terrible pain, like he was near death and just couldn't take it anymore.

I opened my eyes again to see who it was. I couldn't believe it. It was Tony. Anthony, "The Untouchable".

What in the world is he doing in the infirmary? Furthermore, what is he doing in here balling like a baby?

He was curled up in his bed, holding his stomach. I didn't know what could have happened. I thought to myself that no one is crazy enough to attack him. Even if four or five guys attacked him, out of sheer fear, everyone else around would come to his rescue. Everyone knew that if you didn't, and if he survived the attack, he would kill whoever attacked him plus whoever stood by and watched. This man had more power in Greens than the Warden.

Just then the door opened. It was lunchtime and they were serving the food to whoever could eat. I watched the inmate serve the food with my eyes half opened. He went bed to bed dropping off the trays. When he came to Tony's bed, he pulled a tray from the bottom of the cart. When he walked over to his bed he pulled the wrapper off the tray. I noticed as he pulled the wrapper up, it was marked with a black X going across the middle of the wrapper. I blew it off as him getting special treatment, even in the infirmary. Well, I guess that happens when you run the prison.

I lay in the bed for a couple more hours, trying to go back to sleep. Anthony cried for about another hour and a half. After that, I guess he fell asleep or just ran out of tears. I wasn't going to check. I was trying to stay in bed as long as I could.

I let my mind drift for a while. I thought about Crystal when she was a baby. I thought about the times that she made me smile. I thought about her favorite pink little dress that she loved to wear. It had two pink bows on the sleeves and one big pink bow that was on the back.

Just as I started to feel at peace, I heard someone coming towards me. It was the nurse and I guess she was checking up on me. I lay as still as I could, trying not to flinch or change my breathing pattern.

She walked over and I could feel her just staring at me. She rolled something over to my bed and started to pull at the bandage on my neck. I could hear her whispering to herself.

"It's coming through," she said, poking at my neck.

She started to pull the bandage off my neck. It would have been okay if it weren't taped on. I made it through the front side of my neck, but when she snatched it off the back of my neck, I had to scream.

"Oh my goodness, I am so sorry."

"It is okay."

"I thought you were still unconscious. You were out of it for about two days. You lost too much blood."

"I guess I am still losing blood," I said as I felt the blood running down my neck.

"It is okay. I will get that."

She cleaned me up and put a fresh wrapping on my neck. This time she just wrapped it around my neck, no tape.

She was an older woman, maybe around fifty to sixty years old. She had short white hair that barely touched her shoulders and looked to weigh about a hundred pounds soak and wet.

She must have been new here. I had never seen her before, and besides, she was too nice to have been a regular. I guess the more you are here, the more your human side fades and reality sets in; the reality that we are all criminals.

"The police was here yesterday. They wanted to talk to you about what happened."

"Really," I replied, trying to sound interested. I really didn't care. I am in prison for the rest of my life as it is, what are they going to do, give me another life sentence. I never understood that. What would they do, let me die, come back to life and then put me back into jail.

"Really," she said as she took all of the old bloody bandages and put them on her cart. "Now just relax and don't move too much. Let the wound heal up."

"Thank you," I said as she walked off. She stopped in her tracks and walked back over to me.

"Do you know that you are the first person to say 'thank you' to me since I've been here?"

I just stared at her and smiled. I knew how it felt to work a "thankless" job and to feel unappreciated.

"Well, you deserve more than a thank you, but that is all I have right now."

"That is more than enough," she said with a smile. She walked over to my food tray and brought it over to me. As she sat the tray down, she noticed the kitchen's added ingredients.

"That is disgusting. Who would do something like that?" she asked as she picked the tray back up. "Let me get you some more suitable food." She took the tray and walked off. She walked through the door down the hallway and closed it behind her.

I sat up in my bed, excited about the possibility of getting some untainted food. My neck was stiff and sore, and still bleeding from the knife wound.

I looked around the infirmary for a minute. Suddenly, I heard a voice.

"They are gunning for you, Son." I turned my body to the right to see Tony sitting up in his bed looking at me. "I have never seen someone go through as much as you are going through, and I have been here for a long time. What'd you do?"

"I am sure that you have heard by now."

"Yeah, I heard a lot of things, but I want to hear it from you. What'd you do?"

"Nothing."

He laughed a little, held his stomach, and then said, "Okay, what they say you did?"

"Kill my five year old daughter."

"Did you?"

"No, but I don't think anyone cares."

Anthony grabbed his lunch tray that has been sitting for about four hours now. They served spaghetti again. He knew the food was cold, but I don't think he cared.

"Do you mind if I eat this? I understand you killed two inmates over spaghetti."

I laughed a little. "Go ahead, chief."

He grabbed his tray, put salt and pepper on his spaghetti, and looked at me. "If you did it, then you deserve everything that you are getting."

I looked at him in the eyes, breaking all prison laws, and said, "Agreed."

He started to spin his fork in the spaghetti. The noodles were hard and stiff, so it wasn't collecting on the fork as it was supposed to. He looked at me and caught me staring at his food.

"The nurse is coming back with your food, can I have mine?"

"Don't eat it."

"What?"

"Hold your tray up into the light." There was a window right behind his bed where the sun was shining through. He held up the tray into the light.

"That is the salt," he said with a look of concern.

"That is glass. Look at the way the light is reflecting off of it."

He stared at the plate for about two minutes, moving it up and down in the light.
He stuck his finger onto what he thought was salt.

"Son of a ...."

Before he could finish his sentence, the door opened and the nurse walked back into the room. She walked in just in time to see Tony's tray go flying across the room and him go into a rage. She ran over to his bed and tried to calm him down.

"Settle down, settle down. What is wrong, dear?"

Tony stopped yelling and cursing and looked at her.

"Get out, NOW," he shouted at her.

"No, I will not. Not until you tell me what's the matter."

I tried to jump in to save the nurse. "Anthony, she is new here. She doesn't know."

"Did I ask you?" he said, turning his head toward me with pure anger in his eyes. I didn't say anything. I lowered my head like a lion or dog that did not want to fight. He looked back at her. "Get out!"

I looked up at her and pleaded, "Just go, please, just go."

She put my food down on my bed and walked away. Spaghetti was all over the floor by Anthony's bed, but she walked right past it like it wasn't there. I felt really bad for her. She was new; she didn't know any better. She didn't know the animals that she was dealing with. Maybe that was why all of the nurses who had been at Greens for a while acted the way they did. They knew who they were dealing with, so they blocked all emotion and all feelings; that way they couldn't get hurt.

Anthony sat on his bed, heated. I heard him cursing to himself. Somebody was going to pay for what happened and I didn't want it to be me.

Before I could turn back over and try to go to sleep, he spoke. "How did you know?"

"They have been putting stuff in my food for two years. Everything I get, I check and double check. I just looked at your food and something didn't look right."

Just then, the door opened. It was dinnertime and they started to make the rounds in the infirmary. The same guy walked in and started to serve the meals. He went from bed to bed serving each inmate. He walked up to Anthony's bed and again reached to the bottom of the cart. He pulled out a tray, but this time he removed the wrapper before he brought it to him. He walked over keeping his eyes towards the ground and gave the food to Anthony.

"Take the wrapper," I said to Anthony.

"What wrapper?" he asked me, looking confused.

"The wrapper in his hand that he took off your tray when he was standing at the cart."

The guy looked up the way four year olds look when you catch them doing something they had no business doing. He started to walk away.

Anthony yelled, "HEY, let me see the wrapper!"

"What wrapper?"

"The one that is in your hand," I said, trying to help him remember and trying to make sure that he was not going to get out of this.

The guy turned around and started to walk away again.

"HEY, bring me the wrapper, the plastic wrapper that was over the tray!" The guy just stood there. He didn't know what to do. "Son I swear, if you don't bring me the wrapper I will bury you!"

The guy walked over to Anthony and dropped the wrapper on his bed. Anthony opened it up and looked at it.

"What does this X mean?"

"It means that tray was made specifically for you. Your lunch tray wrapper was marked with the same X."

Anthony looked at the guy. He was standing next to his bed, shaking like a leaf in a tornado.

Before Anthony could say a word, he blurted out, "They told me to deliver the marked tray to you."

"They who?"

"The people in the kitchen. They handed me two trays and told me to give the one marked with the black X to you and the red X to him," he said, pointing his finger at me.

"Okay," Anthony said, shaking his head.

"Please don't kill me. I was just the delivery boy. I didn't know what was in the food. I thought that you just had a special order, you know, being who you are and all."

"That is BS," Anthony and I said at the exact same time, though he said the extended version. Both Anthony and the guy looked at me. "If you thought that there was nothing wrong with the food, you wouldn't have been scared to give up the wrapper."

"Exactly," Anthony said, cosigning my observation.

The guy looked at me with anger and frustration in his face, as if he was thinking, "Why are you trying to kill me?" I didn't care. He had been delivering spit on, pissed on and whatever else they could think of food to me every time I was in the infirmary. He knew what they did to the food and I would bet anything that he put some of his own flavor in the food. He had been known to masturbate a lot.

The guy turned and walked away. He didn't have anything to say; what could he say?

"Have a nice life," Anthony said as he walked away. The guy knew what that meant. Heck, I even knew what that meant. When Anthony got out of the infirmary, he is as good as dead.

The next couple of days we just sat and rested, without really speaking to each other. The nurse walked in and just did her job. Her smile was replaced by a stone face. She had been broken in here at Greens and her happiness was replaced with anger; her compassion was gone. She was officially a prison nurse.

Anthony and I were released on the same day. My neck was good enough to go back into population, which meant that it had stopped bleeding. Anthony's stomach problems went away as soon as he discovered the source of the problem.

We walked back into population during free time. Anthony turned to me and said one thing, "A life for a life."

He didn't say anything more and just walked away. Before I could even get back to my cell, the guards stopped me.

"The police would like to talk to you."

They put handcuffs on me once again and walked me to a small room. It must have been the interrogation room. They sat me down, removed the handcuffs and walked out of the room. Moments later, Maria walked in. She sat down in front of me and just stared at me for about two minutes.

"What?" I asked out of curiosity. She didn't answer; she just looked at me.

"What?" I repeated.

"Why did you lie to me?" she asked.

"Lie to you about what?" I inquired.

She stood up and put her face about two inches away from my face. "You said that you didn't kill her. You said that you couldn't kill her."

"I didn't kill her." I responded.

"Then how come I just heard that you murdered two inmates over spaghetti?"

I have always loved how a story could get twisted around to make it whatever the teller liked it to be. I mean, a man could steal a coat with fifty thousand dollars in it. The person he stole it from could find him and kill him for stealing the coat and his money. But then on the news, they say, "Man killed another man over a coat." Then everyone in America sits back and says how bad this world has become, but they are never given the whole story.

She continued, "Killing someone over spaghetti? I mean, how petty is that? And you expect me to believe that you wouldn't lose your temper and do something to that little girl, that you are not capable of something like that? You are a liar. You are a piece of..." She stopped herself and lowered her head.

I laughed as she tried to regain her composure. She looked at me like she wanted to shoot me.

"Is something funny?" she asked, letting her emotions get the best of her and talking heavily with her accent.

"They told you it was over spaghetti? That is funny, that is real funny."

"Well, what was it over?" she asked as she sat down and began to look like she was paying close attention.

I sat up in the chair. If she wanted the story, if she wanted the so-called truth, she was going to get it.

"When you gave me that picture, I hid it. I kept it on me at all times and didn't let it out of my sight. I looked at it everyday, all day. It made the days brighter and the nights just a little bit warmer. Somehow they found out about the picture."

"Who are 'they'?" she asked.

"I don't know who 'they' are, to be honest with you."

"Then how do you know that 'they' found out?"

"Because in the middle of the night, 'they' ran into my cell, beat me, and took the picture out of my pocket. Somebody found out about the picture and they didn't like the fact that I had something to make me smile, something that made me happy. So, they took my picture, my only sign of life left."

"So you killed them for taking a picture? I would have given you another picture."

"I don't know if they took the picture or not; that wasn't the reason why I killed them."

"That is stupid. So you killed them for no reason whatsoever. You don't even know if they took it or not, yet you killed them anyway." She started to speak in Spanish with anger in her voice. I could only imagine what kind of names she was calling me.

"Look, despite what you may feel, they deserved to die."

She screamed at me, "FOR WHAT, because someone took a picture?"

My frustration level had reached its point with her and this whole conversation.

"LOOK, I don't care what you feel about me or what I did. I have been beaten, punched, slammed, smacked, kicked, stabbed, sliced, stomped and everything else you can think of for the last two and a half years. I have been in the infirmary so much that I know all the nurses and most of the doctors by their first names. They have tried to kill me since I've been here. You don't know how it feels to wake up in the middle of the night to four men pulling you off of the top of a bunk bed. You don't know how it feels to have stab wounds on every inch of your body. You don't know about anything that I am going through for something that I didn't do. Yes, they deserved to die and a lot more of them deserve to die."

"Does that mean you have more to kill? You know, by law I am required to report things like that."

"Report it, I don't care."

She stared at me like she was lost. She really didn't know what to say to me.

I looked back at her and asked, "Why are you here?"

She shook her head from side to side softly and responded, "I don't know."

"What do you want from me?"

"I don't know."

"There has to be a reason that you are here. I am sure you just don't come visit convicted murders."

"I am here because I want to believe." Okay, that answer officially came out of nowhere.

"Believe in what?"

"Believe that the man who called me for those two weeks actually exists. That every time you called, it was for real, it wasn't some performance. That you didn't call me everyday just so that you could say it in court, just in case you got caught. I need to believe that you loved Crystal that much."

Not knowing what to say to something like that, I just sat there and looked at her. No words that I could say would ever change her mind, one way or the other.

Maria said, "I want to tell you something and if you tell anyone, I will kill you myself."

I laughed a little bit.

"I am serious, I will kill you," she insisted.

"Who am I going to tell?" I asked.

"No one, because I will kill you."

"Okay, I will not tell anyone."

"Promise me," she said with a very serious look on her face.

"I promise," I said, holding my hand in the air.

"You promise what?"

"Woman, I am sure that your visitation time is almost up. If you are going to tell me something, you might want to get on with it."

She sat back into her chair and responded, "We have plenty of time. They think I am investigating the murder of William Banks. He was killed three years ago and I think you might know something about it. I am a Detective, Jim. That's what I do, investigate."

"Yes, I know, Detective Diaz."

She looked at me with a sort of fear in her eyes. She took a deep breath and slowly started to speak.

"Seven years ago my husband left me. He cheated on me with another woman and ran off to be with her. I was pregnant at the time. Needless to say, the whole situation stressed me, stressed me a lot. I had a miscarriage. My baby died four months before she was due to be born."

Tears came to her eyes as she continued to speak. "I hated him for that. I still do. I just can't believe that a man could care so little for his child that he would just leave. I heard from some mutual friends that he was thrilled when he found out about the miscarriage. He felt like he was off the hook and that he could be with his mistress and not have to deal with me ever again."

She paused for a moment to collect her thoughts. "When I became a police officer a couple of years later, some of my duties were to track down deadbeat dads and serve them papers or lock them up for not paying child support. Needless to say, my impression of fathers in this city wasn't high in the least, until I met you," she said looking at me with half a smile. "For those two weeks, you convinced me that there were and still are fathers out here who actually care about their children; and I just need for that to remain real. I need for that to be true."

I looked at her with sorrow in my eyes and compassion in my heart. I mean, who would want to hurt and leave such a beautiful woman. Now I know that some women are crazy and worth leaving, but not her. She didn't fit the bill of a crazy woman. She wanted love and to believe in love so much that she was sitting there talking to me to make sure that it existed.

"I am sorry," I said as I shook my head in disbelief. "I can't believe that he would do something like that to you."

"It is okay," she said while looking into her purse for some tissue.

"Is there anything that I can do?"

"Just tell me the truth. Tell me the truth about Crystal."

I lowered my head. "Detective Diaz…"

She cut me off, "Maria."

I looked at her and smiled, "Maria, the last time I saw Crystal I was standing at the bottom of the steps in my house. I had just pinched her; she started crying and walked upstairs to get into the shower."

Then it hit me. That was the last time I saw her. Crystal died thinking that I was mad at her. She died thinking that I was upset with her. I just realized that the last time I saw her, my last words weren't 'I love you.' The last thing I said to her was 'take a shower.' I broke down and started crying. I was bawling like a little girl.

Maria stood up and walked over to me. She wrapped her arms around me and just held me. I just cried and cried.

I think at that moment it sunk in to Maria that I didn't kill Crystal. She knew it. She felt the love that I had for Crystal, that I still had for Crystal.

She gave me some tissue that she had in her purse and sat back down. Now was *my* turn to try to regain my composure. I quickly pulled myself together and started to talk again.

"Maria, I killed those men because they mocked the picture. They made fun of Crystal. They made fun of me. They may not have been the ones who took the picture, but they saw it."

Maria looked away. I didn't think she knew what to say.

"I love her. She is all I have. Even though she is dead, she is still in my heart. She will always be a part of me."

"I know."

"And I didn't kill her."

"Yeah, I know."

"You know?" I looked at her, surprised.

"It is just a feeling I have. I could be wrong, but it doesn't seem like you could have done something like that. At least, not to her."

Maria's cell phone rang. She excused herself from the table and went to stand in the corner. She answered her phone, talked for about forty-five seconds and then hung up. She walked back over to the table.

"I have to go."

"I was wondering when your man was going to call you," I said in a joking way. I was really trying to get information on her social life. I knew I was in prison and really didn't have anything to offer; but you only get a certain amount of opportunities in life, so why waste them?

"That was my captain, not my man," she said as she started to gather all of her stuff together.

"I am sorry, I was just trying to make a joke."

She looked at me like I was crazy and explained, "Jim, I am a Detective. No question is just a question. No statement is just a statement. You wanted to know if that was my man or if I have a man?"

I just stared at her because I didn't really know what to say, but I may have just figured out why her husband left her. She was too smart. She knew the games that he played and he couldn't get over on her. She was miles ahead of that guy and was probably telling him what he was going to do before he did it. He couldn't take that, so he left. I was sure she saw it coming, but just because you know something is going to happen, it doesn't make it any easier to deal with.

Maria was finished getting her things together and was getting ready to walk out of the door.

"Thank you for coming to see me," I said just before she banged on the door to be released. "And thank you for believing me."

Maria turned around and said, "Thank you for giving me something to believe in."

She banged on the door and the guards came to let her out. As she was walking out, she turned back and looked at me.

"And the answer to your joke is no, I don't," she said with a smile and walked away.

11

A week had passed since the last time I saw Maria. Ever since I came back from that meeting with her, everything had been different. I don't get attacked anymore. As a matter of fact, everyone had pretty much left me alone. The guards didn't bother me anymore and I could even close my eyes in the shower. I hadn't really washed my face in Greens for over two years because I was afraid to blink.

I could eat the food, if it could be called that. The kitchen staff was fired when Anthony got out of the infirmary and when I say fired, that is exactly what I mean, fired. He or someone he knew had every one of their beds set on fire during the night. With seven or eight cells on fire at once, the guards didn't know what to do. Being that the prison was on graveyard shift, they didn't have enough help to do anything. With the new kitchen staff and the newly found peace for me, my food came to me unflavored. After a couple of days of the food, though, I realized I really hadn't missed anything.

Anthony was talking to me by this time on a regular basis. I didn't know if it was because I pointed out the glass in his food, because I didn't inform anyone that he might have been responsible for the cookout or because he believed that I really didn't kill Crystal. But I wasn't about to complain. I had the King of Greens as an associate, dare I say, a friend; and I didn't care how it had happened.

Everything changed except one thing. The war that I started before I went into the infirmary was still on. I hope that they didn't think because they backed off that I was going to do the same thing.

Two days after the meeting, I found one of my regular attackers in the weight room alone. He was bench-pressing around two hundred and fifty pounds; that was a warm-up for him. He did about fifteen reps and put the weight back on the bar.

As soon as he sat up to stretch his arms, a twenty-five pound weight smacked him in the face from his right side. He fell backwards and off the left side of the bench. I walked around to the left side and smacked him in the back of his head as he was trying to pull himself up. He fell back down to the ground as I slammed the weight into his head again. He just laid there as I repeatedly smashed the weight into his skull.

After about the twentieth time, I heard a voice from the door. "Son, I think he is dead."

It was Anthony, just standing there watching me.

"I know," I said as I slammed the weight down for about the twenty-first time.

"How many times are you going to hit him?"

"Once for every time he tried to rape me."

I kept hitting his head as Anthony stood at the door. Blood was going everywhere, but he didn't appear to care. I hit him about fifteen more times before Anthony spoke again.

"I really hate to break this up, but there is nothing left to hit."

"There is a little more left," I said, as I slammed the weight down again.

"Son," Anthony said as he looked at me. He looked at me in a way that told me to stop.

"Alright," I said as I threw the weight to the side. "Last one."

I walked over to the stacked weights and grabbed a forty-five pound weight. I walked over to his body and slammed down the weight on the remains of his head. The weight fell flat, crushing anything left.

"I guess that was for the one time he succeeded," Anthony said.

"Yeah, that faggot got me," I said. I felt shameful for it; but when it was five against one, how much could I have done? I fought as hard as I could.

"Are you done?"

"With him, yes. I have to get two more, at least two that were connected with him. It *was* four, but someone invited two of them to a barbeque."

Anthony looked at me and laughed, "Yeah, a barbeque. I wonder who was nice enough to do that."

I looked at him with a smile and answered, "I have no idea. I don't know anything and I don't appreciate this line of questioning."

Anthony laughed and said, "Keep it that way. If you don't know anything, then I don't know anything," he said as he pointed to my hands.

I looked down to see the blood dripping from my hands, looked back at him and said, "Yeah, we'll keep it that way."

The very next day I was able to get the next two, one in the morning before breakfast and one in the courtyard during exercise. It is funny that they were both alone, and both times Anthony was there watching. I never asked him why he was there, but I did thank him for arranging my little "meetings" with the inmates. He never took credit for it, but I knew that he had set everything up.

Things settled down a little bit for the rest of the week. I didn't kill anyone else and no one messed with me. As crazy as it sounds, once I got past all of the chaos, prison life wasn't that bad. Don't get me wrong. It sucked in there, but compared to what I was going through at first, it seemed like I just entered paradise.

"You have a visitor," the guard said as he walked up to my cell.

"Who?"

"Some cop."

I got up so that he could cuff me. Once he put the cuffs on me, he took to me to the prison's interrogation room.

He left and lo and behold, Maria walked in.

I looked at her, smiled and declared, "You miss me."

She looked at me, stone-face. She was pissed off.

"Jim, what in the…?" she paused and said, "What are you doing?"

"Nothing, I am sitting here."

"You know what I mean. What are you doing in here?"

I just stared at her. I knew what she was talking about, but I was not going to just volunteer information.

"Okay, you lost me."

"Jim, I just received information about three inmates who were killed last week. What are you doing? Are you trying to die in prison?"

"Maria, in case you didn't know, I am in prison for life anyway. I will never get out. So, if I did happen to kill someone, what difference would it make?"

"If you happened to kill someone? What do you mean 'if'? You already told me you did!"

"Well, I really couldn't deny the incident in the cafeteria. It is kind of hard to say that I didn't do something when everyone saw me, you know?"

She just looked at me, at a loss for words.

"And why are you getting reports on what is going on here? You wouldn't have any jurisdiction here."

"I was interested in one of the inmates here, so I requested a report of any and every thing that happened in Greens."

"So you have been checking up on me? You know that is stalking."

"Investigating, Jim, I call it investigating."

We just sat and soaked in the moment. It just felt good to have someone care about you. I hadn't had that in a long time.

"Where is Emily?" she said.

You know, after all of this time, that is the one thing that really never crossed my mind. Where in the world is Emily? I hadn't seen her in over two and a half years. She had just disappeared on me.

"I don't know. I haven't seen her since a week after Crystal left."

"Are you serious? She didn't come to court or visit you here?"

"Yes, I am serious and no, she didn't."

Maria looked at me like she felt sorry for me. She must have known how hard it had been for me; and for my so-called wife not to be there for me, she thought it was like salt on the wound. If she only knew that until this moment I really hadn't realized Emily was gone, she might have felt a little different.

"I can't believe that she hasn't contacted you in some way. She hasn't attempted to write you or call you?"

"No," I said, showing as little emotion as possible.

"And you don't care?"

"Not really. I mean after every thing that I went through and everything that I am still going through, do you really think I have time to worry about Emily and where she is?"

"I guess not, but that is still your wife."

I looked at her with a bit of anger in my face. I responded, "Wife? Don't ever associate me with that woman using that word. She's my daughter's mother, sure, but not my wife."

Maria was stuck for a moment; she really didn't know what to say. She just looked at me for awhile. She didn't say anything; she just stared at me. Finally, she grabbed a folder out of her briefcase and slid the folder to me.

I opened the folder and looked inside. It contained two pictures of Crystal. One with Crystal sitting on her first bike and one with Emily sitting next to Crystal on a bench in the park that was down the street from our house.

I took the picture of Crystal on her bike out of the folder and slid the folder back to Maria.

"Thank you. You know, I love to look at her. She was so beautiful. It's just..." I trailed off as I tried to fight back the tears. I had cried enough over her, but I still couldn't help getting choked up when I saw her. "I will never see her graduate from kindergarten or high school. I will never see her get married. I will never see her smile again. I will never hear her laugh." I wiped the tears away from my eyes. "I am sorry, but I just miss her so much."

"It is okay Jim. I am sorry, but that picture is not yours."

"What?"

Maria didn't say anything. She just looked at me and held her hand out. I put the picture in her hand and she put it back into the folder.

"Well, I have been here long enough. I have to go. Please don't make me come back because I got another report about you - I mean, about Greens."

I looked at her and smiled. "So your reports are about me?" I asked.

She grabbed her stuff and walked to the door, "Bye, Jim."

"Bye, Maria."

12

Four years had passed since I had been convicted of the murder of Crystal Sutton, my baby. Maria had been to see me at least two to three times a week for the past year. At first, she had come every now and then saying that she was trying to make sure I didn't kill someone just to see her.

Now, she doesn't make excuses to come see me. She has been here so much that when she comes, the guards tell me that my girlfriend is visiting. I told her that they called her that and she just smiled and said something in Spanish. I didn't have a clue what she said, but she smiled while she said it. I didn't think it could have been that bad.

From that day on, I called her my girlfriend and she would say whatever she always said in Spanish. At first I would just say it to flirt, but eventually it took on a more serious tone for me. I used to get depressed about it because I really didn't have anything to offer her; but Anthony reminded me that she never asked me for anything and that she knew the situation.

My war with the inmates died down at about the three and a half year mark. Around that time, a war between Anthony and everyone else started. The "Supremacy" group and the "Muslim" group decided to work together to get rid of the King.

The only problem for them was that he really *was* like a King. He moved where others couldn't. The guards were under his rule, so he could move throughout the prison at will. Nobody could compete with that. They had to play by the rules and he didn't.

So while they attacked him during the day in the courtyard, in the cafeteria or in the shower, he attacked them throughout the night. When the war started, both groups had about five hundred members a piece. When the war ended, there weren't fifty members between the two groups. He, or shall I say we, killed about two to three of them a night. The barbeque that the kitchen staff was a part of looked like a snowball fight compared to what they went through. They really didn't stand a chance; and the more we killed, the more members quit.

After the war was over the prison went back to normal, if you could call it that. The guards went back to being guards, at least on the surface, and the inmates went back to being inmates.

The four year mark changed my life forever. It marked the biggest conversation of my life.

Anthony and I were walking in the courtyard. We were just making casual conversation. Then he just asked me out of nowhere, "Son, seriously, did you kill her?"

I stopped walking and looked at him. The question caught me off guard. We hadn't talked about that since the infirmary. "No," I responded.

Anthony started walking again and I started to walk with him. He stopped, looked at me and spoke again.

"Are you finished?"

I knew what he meant. This was his way of asking if I still had unfinished business with anyone else in the prison.

"Yes," I said. My answer caught *him* off guard. I guess he expected for me to be done, but I had one more thing to do. "Who took my picture?"

Anthony looked at me like he saw a ghost. I guess he thought I forgot about that. He just stood there for a moment. I could only imagine that he was searching for the correct words to say.

"Anthony, who took my picture?" I demanded.

He turned around and pointed at a guard who was standing against the wall. Then he pointed to another guard who was standing on the tower watching over the courtyard. Lastly, he pointed to another guard who stood against the fence.

"And who gave the order for them to do it?"

Anthony just stood there, not saying anything.

"I want them alone; then I will be done."

"You got it," Anthony said without hesitation. "But make it quick, none of that blow for blow garbage. Hit them and move."

"You got it," I said and walked away.

Anthony stood there, looking around. I could only assume he was thinking about how to get the guards alone. They were never alone. The King was really going to have to work his magic on this one; but he owed me and he knew it.

That night, I woke up to the sound of my cell door opening. Uncle Don just laid in his bed. He couldn't run or move if he wanted to because he was paralyzed from the waist down. Anthony said I couldn't kill him, so I just took his legs for what he did.

Three men rushed in and grabbed me out of my bed. They handcuffed me and started to beat me. They got in about eight or nine good shots then dragged me out of my cell. They took me to the laundry room and threw me in the middle of the floor. I was bent over on my knees in the middle of a huge laundry room. They locked the doors so no one could get in. Just then, Anthony walked from around the dryer and looked at me.

"Take the cuffs off," he ordered the guards. One of the guards walked over and removed the cuffs, but he made sure he kicked me in the stomach before he did.

Anthony walked up to me. "I gave the order," he said right before he punched me in my face, sending me to the ground. He jumped on top of me and grabbed me by the throat. He started to choke me. I fought and fought until I was able to roll him off of me. I got up and tried to crawl away. I could hardly fight Anthony one on one, let alone one on four. Anthony got up and ran over to me. He jumped on my back and we started to roll around on the ground, crashing into a washing machine. The crash took a lot out of Anthony and he let me go.

I got up and tried to get away. I ran over to the other side of the laundry room as the guards chased me. They caught up to me and attacked me while Anthony laid next to the washing machine.

Screams were echoing throughout the laundry room. Then all of a sudden, the screams stopped. There was nothing but silence.

Anthony got up off the ground as a figure walked towards him. It was extremely dark, so he couldn't see who was coming. As the figure entered the light, he saw that it was me with blood all over my shirt and face and a knife in my hand.

Anthony just stared at me for a minute, then spoke, "I said make it quick."

"I did."

"Are they dead?"

"If they aren't, they soon will be." I figured that if the stab wounds didn't kill them, they would bleed to death by the time they were discovered.

Anthony reached into his pocket and pulled out a picture. It was the picture of Crystal eating spaghetti.

"Hold onto it for me," I said as he held it out to me. "At least until I get cleaned up."

"You got it."

As we walked out of the laundry room and back to our cells, Anthony asked me, "Are you done?"

"Yeah, I'm done."

13

The next day the entire prison was on lock down. They discovered the bodies of the three guards and shut everything down. We didn't even go to breakfast and lunch didn't look too promising either.

I guess the Warden was pretty upset about three of his guards getting stabbed to death in a laundry room. He ordered that all of the blood at the scene be tested along with every inmate to see if they could find a match. They did. They found my blood at the scene, the blood from the punch that Anthony gave me.

The Warden decided to have me charged with murder in the first degree of three correctional officers. He wanted the death penalty and he got the perfect prosecutor to push for it. Scott Wilcox, my public defender, was now working for the district attorney's office representing the State. He wanted me dead more than anyone. When my case came across his desk, he probably jumped at the opportunity to have me sentenced to death.

I went to the hole for three months, one month for every guard who was killed. I knew that it was supposed to be more, but I thought Anthony must have thrown his weight around and gotten it reduced.

It was my first day back in population and I already had a visitor. I thought it was Maria; I hoped that it was Maria. They took me to a small room in the prison and told me to wait there. I sat with great anticipation as I waited for Maria to open the door. The door finally opened and all of my hopes were crushed, or so I thought.

A man walked in. He was a short, fat white man with brown hair going around the sides of his head, with a bald spot on top. He had on a grey suit with a white shirt and blue tie.

He walked to the table and flung his briefcase onto it. He sat down in front of me, reached into his pocket to grab his glasses, and opened his briefcase.

"Mr. Sutton, Jim Sutton," he said with a hint of a New York accent.

"Yes, I am."

"You are being charged with the murder of three Correctional Officers," he said as he flipped through a folder. "Let me see, how can we get you out of this?" He continued to look through the folder.

"Who are you?" I asked out of sheer curiosity.

"I am your lawyer, Mr. Sutton."

"Are you like a public defender, because my last public defender wanted me killed?"

"Well, Mr. Sutton, I am not a public defender. I get paid four hundred dollars an hour and rest assured, I do not want you dead."

My jaw dropped as I said, "Four hundred dollars an hour, I can't afford that."

"Don't worry about that. We can take care of that later."

"Later?" I asked questioning his sanity. I was locked up for life, what 'later' was he waiting on?

"Yes sir, later. Now, let's go over what happened." He took out a voice recorder, hit record, and put it on the table. Then he took out a pad and pen and prepared to write.

"Okay," I said, still focused on the 'later'.

"Okay, why were you out of your cell?"

"They brought me out."

"Who are 'they', the guards?"

"Yes, they came into my cell during the night. They handcuffed me and took me to the laundry room."

"Did they hit you?"

"Yes, they hit me in my cell, on the way to the laundry room, and in the laundry room."

"What happened in the laundry room?"

"I was attacked, I defended myself and now I am here," I said, trying not to give up too much information. It had all been a setup, they were just dumb enough to fall for it.

"Mr. Sutton, I am going to need a little bit more information than that."

"What would you like to know, sir?"

"What happened?"

"I just told you what happened."

He took his glasses off. He grabbed the tape recorder and hit the stop button. He got up and walked to the door. He stretched up on his toes and looked around out of the window in the door. He walked back over to me and whispered.

"The only way I can help you is if you tell me the truth. You have got to tell me what happened from beginning to end. If you don't, there is nothing I can do for you."

"So, you want me to trust you?"

"You have no other choice."

"Well, the last lawyer I had attempted to kill me on more than one occasion. So, forgive me for not running to you with open arms and loose lips."

He stood there for a second and reasoned, "Jim, let's look at your options here. Right now, if you don't get good representation, you are going to die. The State will do everything in their power to make sure you are put to death. As a matter of fact, even if you get good representation, you are pretty much going to be put to death. The only way you will beat this is to have the best, and I am the best."

He sat back down in his seat. "You did it. I know you did it; you know you did it. Everyone in Greens knows you killed those guards. So, unless you let me help you, you will die, sooner than later."

I lowered my head. I really didn't have much to live for, but that didn't mean I was ready to die. It seemed like he was the only way for me to extend my pointless life.

"What do you want to know?"

He hit the record button on the tape recorder and laid it back down on the table.

"What happened?"

"That night I was awakened when my cell door opened."

"Why did your cell door open?"

"So the three guards could come in there and get me."

He wrote down something on his notepad.

"Continue."

"That night I was awakened when my cell door opened. They ran into my cell, pulled me off of the top of my bed and put handcuffs on me. After they put the handcuffs on me, they started to kick and punch me."

"Did they tell you why they put the handcuffs on you?"

"No, they didn't say a word."

"Did you resist in any way?"

"No, not at all. I was used to the nightly visits. It happened a lot during my first couple of years here at Greens. Normally, I would just curl up and try to protect myself."

"Okay," he said as he stopped the tape. He hit the rewind button and then stopped it. "Leave that part out. Do not bring up the nightly visits. Do not bring up the fact that you were attacked before."

"Why?"

"Because you cannot prove without a shadow of a doubt that these were the guys who attacked you at night. If we make it seem like it was just some random event, the jury will believe that you were scared. If they think that you went through this all of the time, they are going to think that you were out for revenge. Scared equals self-defense; revenge equals murder; murder, in turn, equals death for you."

There was not really much I could say after that but that this guy was a freaking genius. If he truly did charge four hundred an hour, he was worth every penny; I could see that and I hadn't even talked to him for thirty minutes yet.

"Now, start back at the cell and pick it up from there," he said as he hit play and put the recorder back on the table.

"Okay, they put the handcuffs on me, beat me, then dragged me to the laundry room."

He questioned, "Why did they take you to the laundry room? And what happened when you entered the laundry room?"

I answered, "They threw me on the floor. I escaped and tried to run away. They ran after me and then I defended myself. The rest you can read about from the report."

"Why did you stab them so many times?" he asked.

"To make sure they were dead."

He stopped the recorder and hit the rewind button. The tape went back for a couple of seconds, he hit stop, then he hit the record button and looked at me.

"Why did you stab them so many times?" he repeated.

"Because they kept coming after me and I was afraid for my life."

He winked at me as he wrote something down on his notepad.

"And where did the knife come from?"

I didn't know what to say to that question. I couldn't explain how I got the knife without bringing up Anthony. I couldn't bring up Anthony because I just couldn't bring up Anthony. I didn't want his name brought up because I didn't want him to be involved in this case in any way.

He looked at me and asked the question again, "Where did the knife come from?"

"I found it in the laundry room." That was the best answer I could come up with.

He stopped the tape and looked at me. "You found it? There just happened to be a knife in the room that three guards took you in, in the middle of the night. It was just conveniently there?"

"Yeah, what are the odds of that happening?" I said, trying to smile and joke it off.

He didn't laugh. He didn't even smile. He stared at me and said, "You set this up, didn't you? You planned for them to take you to the laundry room. They walked right into a trap and didn't even see it. Who else was in on it?"

He put his head down and ran his hands over the top of his head and down the back of his neck. I just looked at him. That was one question I was not going to answer, no matter how much my life was in his hands.

After it became clear that I was not going to answer the 'who else' question, he blurted out, "Good, cause I don't want to know. Okay, let's recap, from the top," he said as he picked up the recorder and hit the rewind button. The tape went all the way back to the beginning. Mr. Sutton, what happened?"

"I was asleep in my cell and was woken up to the sound of my cell door crashing open. Three men rushed in and pulled me out of my bed. They handcuffed me, beat me, and dragged me to the laundry room. There, I can only assume, they were going to kill me. I was able to escape from them for only a second, but they caught up to me."

He stopped the tape and jumped in, "How did you get the handcuffs off?"

I just stared at him again. I didn't know what to say.

"Okay, I see that you are leaving out a big part of this story. That is fine, but if you are going to cover for someone you have to make sure you cover yourself. Everything that you say has to be in line with you being surprised, scared, shocked and thrown into a situation where self-defense was your only option. You getting out of handcuffs when three guards are attacking you is not self-defense. It means that either someone helped you out of the handcuffs or you had a key, and both of those answers don't go well with your self-defense argument. You magically finding a knife doesn't help you either."

He put the tape back to the beginning again, hit record and requested, "Now Mr. Sutton, please tell me what happened."

I started again, "I was asleep in my cell and was awakened when my cell door opened. Three men rushed in and pulled me out of my bed. They beat me and dragged me to the laundry room."

He looked up from his notepad and winked at me.

I continued, "They threw me in the laundry room and locked the door. I couldn't get out. I tried to run away from them, but they caught up to me. They attacked me and I just tried to fight them off."

"And where did the knife come from?"

"It was on the floor in the laundry room. One of the guards could have dropped it."

"And why did you stab them so many times?"

"They kept coming after me. I didn't count how many times I stabbed them, I just knew that they were trying to kill me and I didn't want to die."

He stopped the tape, smiled and said, "Perfect."

He packed up his stuff and told me that he would see me in court.

They took me back to population where I would stay until my trial started. After the meeting I had with him, I really didn't feel worried about the trial anymore. He seemed like he was more than capable of handling this case. For once in the past four years and three months, my mind was at ease.

14

Eleven weeks had passed and the day of my trial arrived. I went to court feeling nervous because this trail could mean death for me. I knew that prison life wasn't the best life, but at least it *was* a life.

I entered the courtroom and was seated next to my lawyer, Paul. When the judge asked how the defense pleaded, he stood up and shouted with fire in his voice, "Not guilty."

The judge looked at him like he was crazy. I think everyone in the courtroom thought he was crazy, but he knew what he was doing. He was like a lion creeping in a field of tall grass. No one ever saw him coming and by the time they did see him, it was too late.

The prosecution's opening argument was that I was a convicted murderer and that it was nothing for me to kill again. I killed three hard-working, dedicated correctional officers who gave their lives upholding justice. He pointed to their families and drilled home the point that their children would finish growing up without a father. Their wives would never see their husbands again. He said I robbed those families when I stabbed them repeatedly without mercy, killing them without compassion like an animal. He stated that if a dog attacked a human, we would put that dog to sleep. Being that I was not acting like a human, but like an animal, then I needed to be put to sleep like an animal.

I laughed to myself. I was expecting Scott to stand up and say, "He did it," and sit back down. I guess he brought his 'A' game to this trial.

Paul turned to me and laughed himself. I knew that he was good, but I really didn't think he could read minds. Paul leaned over to me and whispered in my ear, "Watch this."

Paul stood up and approached the jury. He looked the jury of seven women and five men over. He wanted more women on the jury than men because he said they think with their emotions more; and that was his way to win this case, emotion. He said a woman was more likely to believe that a man was scared than a man would, and he wanted them to believe that I had been scared.

"Ladies and gentlemen, the prosecution is correct. My client acted like an animal," he paused for the effect, "because he was treated as one. They attacked him and they dragged him to a laundry room to slaughter him," again he paused, "like an animal. Everything the prosecution is going to tell you is going to make you hate my client. Everything that he is going to bring up is going to make you wish that Mr. Sutton was dead. Everything that he brings up is going to make you wish that the guards had succeeded in killing this so-called animal." He paused again, "But I want you to remember, it was that same hatred that caused the guards to open his cell door that night. It was that same hatred that caused the guards to attack him. It was that same hatred that made them take him to a closed area so that they could do whatever they planned to do to him. They took him to an area where even if he screamed, no one could hear him."

He looked the jury over for a second. He looked for a reaction from the jury to see if he needed to keep going. I guess he hadn't seen what he wanted to see, because he continued, "If you corner animals, some lay in the corner and wait to be killed, while some animals come out fighting. If that animal would have died in the corner, we wouldn't even be here today. You would be at home or at work and you wouldn't have even cared about the road kill in the back of a prison's laundry room." He stared at them for a second and continued, "But that animal was afraid, afraid for his life, and no matter how little you, the prosecution, or those guards thought of his life, it was still his life. He didn't want to die in the back of a laundry room and he shouldn't be penalized for fighting for his right to live."

The prosecution did just as Paul said he would. Scott brought up my conviction in the first degree murder of Crystal. He brought up the cruelty of her death and the torment that I put her through. He made the jury hate me.

His plan might have worked if Paul hadn't already told them that they were going to hate me. From the beginning, Paul banked on Scott wanting to make the jury hate me. So he approached the trial the same way, making the jury hate me.

Scott brought up forensic evidence that my blood was at the scene. The detective (not Maria though, she never came to the trial) testified that the DNA test proved that I was at the scene of the crime.

Scott thought this was some kind of victory for him and the State, but the only thing it meant was I was there at the scene. I admitted being at the scene. So for him to call a witness just to say I was at the scene was kind of pointless, or so I thought. Paul, on the other hand, loved the fact that he called this witness.

Paul asked him where my blood was located in the laundry room.

He responded, "About twenty-five feet away from the door."

Paul asked, "Was there any other blood in that area?"

He answered, "No."

Paul smiled and said, "So it is safe to assume that is where my client was attacked." The detective didn't say anything. Paul continued, "Where did you find the blood of the officers?"

He stated, "About seventy-five feet away from the door."

Paul asked, "Was Mr. Sutton's blood there also?"

He responded, "Yes, we found traces of Mr. Sutton's blood at that location."

Paul grinned and said, "In a written statement, my client said that he was attacked and when he ran for his life, the guards caught up with him and he just tried to defend himself. Does the evidence at the scene support my client's written statement?"

The detective looked directly at the jury, "No, it doesn't."

Paul asked, "It doesn't? How so?"

"Because he could have cut himself on purpose when walking back to the door."

Paul then asked, "When the medical examiner examined him, did he find any knife wounds on his body?"

"No," the detective said, killing his 'cut himself' theory.

"Did he find any wounds on his body at all?"

"He found bruises on his chest, stomach, arms and back. He also found a gash in his mouth."

Paul looked at the jury, "And I guess that doesn't support the written statement either."

The detective jumped back and exclaimed, "No it doesn't, he could have had himself beaten or could have bruised himself."

I think everyone in the courtroom thought that was the dumbest answer possible. Even the judge lowered his head on that response. Some of the members of the jury looked at him in disbelief, while some looked on in anger.

Scott called some guards that worked at Greens. He asked them what kind of prisoner I was. They brought up the murders of the two inmates in the cafeteria. When one guard brought that up, Paul just looked at me, smiled and said, "You have been busy, I see."

Paul disregarded the murders in the cafeteria, stating that it was a separate case and had nothing to do with this trial. The judge agreed.

Paul's counter to the guards was simple. How in the world did I get out of my cell? One guard said that I could have tried to escape, but the three guards caught me. Paul's question to that was after I defeated the three guards, (making it sound like I was a hero), why didn't I continue my escape? Why did I just return to my cell? The guard couldn't answer that.

After Paul dispatched the witnesses, it was on to the closing arguments. I asked if he wanted me to take the stand. He said I didn't have to, that the case was already won.

The closing arguments were simple, Scott pushed angry and enraged while Paul pushed afraid and scared. The jury believed afraid and scared.

The trial lasted about three days. After the trial, the media conducted interview after interview with the jury. One man from the jury said it all, "After everything that was said, I believe they took him in there to kill him but they just couldn't finish the job."

15

It had been a week since my trial ended. Once I got back to population, Anthony crowned me as an 'Untouchable'. I was a black inmate who killed three white guards and wouldn't serve sixty seconds of jail time for it. Maybe that was what made us 'Untouchable', we could pretty much do what we wanted to do.

Everyday since the end of my trial I had received bags of letters. When I first came to Greens, I received letters everyday. Some from fathers of daughters who were murdered, and they would wish me all of the pain and death the world could offer. Some came from mothers who hated my very existence. They would say how they cried for Emily and Crystal and would pray at night that justice would find me in the form of death.

I think that was the one thing that really pissed me off the most. A woman could kill five of her children and everyone in the world would run to her defense. They would say that she had post-pardom depression and that she didn't know what she was doing, even though she would call the police afterwards or blame a black man for killing the children. They would blame the husband, the doctor, the church, even the children, but never the mother.

On the other hand, if a father happened to beat a child roughly, he was just an abusive, crazy piece of….well, you get the point. To me, that was just maddening.

The letters I received after that trial were different than the letters I received directly before the trial. Before the trial, I received letter after letter stating everyone was happy I was going to get executed. They were happy that justice was finally going to get served.

After that trial, I received bags of letters from people saying how the system was broken. Some even said that they wanted to come to the jail to kill me themselves. Obviously, because the guards were white I received the 'Die Nigger' letters and statements that all black people are animals and deserve to be killed. I even received some letters from black people saying that I was a poor excuse for a black man and I exemplified everything that was wrong with black people as a whole.

All in all, Anthony and I thought it was quite amusing. We would read the letters and laugh to each other. I thought it was funny how everyone was so brave and had so much heart because I was locked behind bars. Everyone loved to talk about what they would do to me, mostly because they believed they would never see me. They believed that I would never get out of prison. Heck, I believed that I would never get out of prison, that is, until my meeting with Paul.

About a month and a half after my trial, guards approached me in the courtyard. Anthony and I found this amusing also because they no longer sent one guard to get me or handcuff me, they sent a mini squad.

They took me to the little room, sat me down and told me to wait. Again, I was hoping that it was Maria, but a part of me knew that it wouldn't be. I hadn't seen her since the laundry room incident, and I didn't think I would be seeing her again. Maybe the incident made her realize that she was dealing with a convicted murderer, and that was killing the very thing she had come to love about me.

Paul walked into the room, all smiles. He sat down at the table across from me, put his briefcase on the table and popped it open.

"Good afternoon, Mr. Sutton. How are you feeling today?"

"Fine Mr. Reed, how about you?"

He took a handkerchief out of his suit pocket to wipe the sweat from his forehead and replied, "Oh, I am okay, just hot."

It was winter time and they had the heat pumping on this side of the prison, which made it really hot.

"Yeah, I know, it *is* hot." I paused for a second as he finished wiping his head. "I really don't mean to sound rude, but do I have another murder charge that came up or are you here for your money?"

"Murder charge yes, my money no."

I shook my head in disbelief. I knew that they never tried me for the cafeteria incident, but come on, it had been over a year and a half now.

Paul pulled a folder out of his briefcase. "You were charged with murder in the first degree, which seems to be a theme with you," he said jokingly.

I wanted to laugh, but the frustration of this situation had reached its breaking point with me. They couldn't get me on the guards, so they were going to try to get me on this. I knew Paul was good, but I was already in jail for life. Just leave me alone already.

Paul started to look over the information in the folder. "So, did you do it?"

"Yeah, I did it."

Paul looked at me surprised and inquired, "You did it?"

I didn't see a tape recorder, so I really didn't understand his answer. Maybe he was trying to prep me already.

"Well, off the record, I really don't know what to say. It really wasn't self-defense. The only thing I can think to go for is insanity, but I really don't know how to play that angle."

Paul looked at me confused and asked, "So, off the record, you did it?"

"Yeah."

Paul grabbed his briefcase and headed for the door, "Good day, Mr. Sutton."

"Wait, what do you want me to say?"

Paul turned around with his face blood-red from anger, "You despicable man, you." He slammed his briefcase on the floor. "I can't believe that you are sitting here telling me that you killed that little girl!"

"Little girl?" I asked really confused. "What little girl? I thought you were talking about the two guys in the cafeteria."

Paul's face softened and went back to its normal color. "I took care of that a while ago. I was talking about Crystal."

I was officially mentally challenged at that time. I felt like my brain came to a complete stop. "Huh....you took care of it?"

Paul picked up his briefcase and walked back to the table. "Yeah, I got that dismissed a while back."

I just stared at him in amazement.

Paul put his briefcase back on the table and sat back down. He pulled the folder out and started flipping through it again.

"Now, let's start over. So, Mr. Sutton, did you do it?"

My brain was still not back on planet Earth, but I did have enough understanding to say, "No sir, I didn't."

"Good, then let me get you out of here. This is no place for a free man to be."

Great, I was just about to get my thoughts together again, and he went and said that.

"Free....who gets free?"

"You do, Mr. Sutton. I will file the paperwork tomorrow. I will try to push for a trial as fast as possible. I do apologize, Mr. Sutton, but it is going to take some time. The courts are extremely slow."

I am still looking at him with a glazed look in my eyes. I couldn't believe he just said that he was going to get me out of here. I wanted to get excited, but after everything I had been through, I really didn't want to get my hopes up to get disappointed.

"You can talk Mr. Sutton, it is okay."

"I really don't know what to say, but thank you."

"You are quite welcome, Mr. Sutton. As a matter of fact, it would be my pleasure to do this for you."

I started to get nervous and asked, "Do you think you can win?"

Paul laughed, "I wouldn't have brought it up if I didn't."

Paul read through the papers in the folder for a little bit, then said, "They never proved anything."

"I know."

He read more, then looked up at me. "Scott was your lawyer," he said, chuckling a little bit with his comment. "Now I know you didn't do it."

"Why is that?" I said out of curiosity.

"Because," he said, wiping his forehead again, "the State gave Scott to all of the defendants that they didn't have evidence on or had a very weak case against. More often than not, he made his clients take a deal. He would make it seem that a deal was their only option. If they were dumb enough to go to court, then he would be the worst possible lawyer in the world to make sure they didn't walk."

I laughed a little bit and asked, "So Scott working for the prosecution is nothing new then?"

"Are you kidding me? He has been working for them ever since he became a public defender. I mean, look at it. He has to have the worst possible record of any lawyer ever, and he got promoted for it."

I sat in my chair, pissed off. I couldn't believe that they set me up like that. I knew that they didn't have anything. I couldn't believe Scott tried to get me killed because I wouldn't take the plea. I couldn't believe that they knew they couldn't convict me, but they did it anyway.

Paul could read my facial expressions and my anger.

"Let it go. All of that is in the past now."

"He is so dead."

Paul laughed out loud and said, "Yeah, that is just the challenge I need - a dead state's attorney. How about we worry about getting you out of here first?"

"Yes, sir."

Paul got up, grabbed his briefcase and banged on the door. "You will be hearing from me shortly. Until then, stay alive and stay out of trouble."

I smiled and replied, "You got it. And again, thank you for doing this."

Paul smiled back and responded, "Hey, a life for a life."

The guard opened the door and let Paul out. The mini squad came, handcuffed me, and took me back to population.

As soon as I got back to population, I ran right up to Anthony. "We have to talk, now."

Anthony dropped his cards on the table and got up. The other inmates who he was playing with didn't even look up. We walked off to the weight room. As soon as we entered, everyone left. We didn't even have to do or say anything, they just walked out.

Anthony looked at me, "What's up?"

"You know Paul, don't you?"

Anthony looked at me with a smile on his face and said, "I might have talked to him before. Why, did he tell you he knew me?"

"No, I just had a meeting with him. At the end of my meeting he said, 'a life for a life.' That is what you said to me when you left the infirmary."

"I might have told him about you. Why, is there something wrong?"

"No, he said that he is going to try to get me out of here."

Anthony's jaw dropped. "What do you mean, get you out?"

"Just that, he said that he is going to file papers tomorrow to appeal my case. But I am not trying to get my hopes up because I know anything can happen. I mean, we can lose the appeal and I will be right back here."

Anthony looked at me with confidence and stated, "You won't lose."

"What? How do you know?"

"Because Paul doesn't lose. I don't think that he has ever lost a case."

Then it hit me, that was what made Anthony 'Untouchable'. He could kill anyone he wanted and Paul could get him off. Anthony wasn't 'untouchable' because he was the biggest or strongest, but because he had the greatest lawyer on the face of this earth.

"So, Paul is what makes you 'Untouchable'?

"Pretty much."

"Then why are you still in here? Why don't you tell him to get you out?"

Anthony lowered his head like a man defeated and answered, "I can't. I did so much dirt on the outside that I couldn't walk down the street without having someone try to kill me. On top of all of the things I did in here, son, I would have thousands of people lined up to take turns shooting me. Plus, if I were to get out, I couldn't go anywhere or do anything. I would just be in prison in my own home. Nope, it is better for me to stay in here. Here I am protected."

There was not really much I could say about that. Here the State thinks they are protecting the world from Anthony, but in reality, they are protecting Anthony from the world.

I guess I understood where he was coming from in a way. In prison he was like a god. He could get what he wanted, when he wanted it. In the streets, it might not have been that easy. As a matter of fact, I knew that it wouldn't have been that easy, and he did too.

For the rest of our free time, we just sat in the weight room talking. We talked about what I was going to do when I got out. He was more excited than I was at first, but then I guess reality hit him. He realized he would be back on his own again. After everything we went through, it was going to be hard for him to be on his own again.

That night I was so excited that I couldn't sleep. My mind was running all over the place. I thought about if I didn't get out. Then I thought about what I was going to do my first day out. I thought about how I was going to eat fast food for three months straight, drink alcohol and just sleep peacefully. Then my mind would switch back to thinking about if I didn't make it out and had to keep eating this same crap for the rest of my life. I tormented myself like this all night, going from extremely happy to suicidal depression. I just couldn't get it out of my mind. Freedom.....I had a real chance at freedom.

16

A couple of months had passed since Paul submitted the appeal. Everything changed once he submitted it. The guards treated me a whole lot differently. I think the possibility of me getting out of jail after killing three guards didn't sit real well with them, but what could they do? I knew that they wanted to kill me, but they knew they would end up in here. A guard turned inmate was like putting a bloody animal in the water - they're lunchmeat.

They also knew that I could eliminate them without serving a minute of jail time for it. I mean, I killed three guards and got off, what was one more?

Then, there was Anthony. He just wasn't the same after I told him that Paul was going to file an appeal for my case involving Crystal. We still talked and everything, but he just seemed depressed. I knew prison wasn't supposed to be the happiest place on earth, but Anthony had never let it get to him; or at least he never showed that it was getting to him. He always kept his head up and his chest out; but for the last couple of months he often held his head down. Sometimes he wouldn't even look me in the eye when we talked. That was very unusual, considering he always had to have eye contact to make sure you were paying attention.

When I first came to Greens, I wanted to be just like him. I envied him because of his toughness and control. Some days I wanted to be like him just so I had the courage to back everyone off of me, other days I wanted to be like him because I felt a person like him would never lose his child. I felt no one in the world would dare cross someone like him.

Who knew that years later, I would pity him? Anthony will always be in prison, physically or mentally. If he decided to stay in prison, he will die in prison. If he decided to let Paul work his magic and get him out, then he would spend the rest of his days chained to the house. Even if no one looked for him, he would always be worried that a son or brother of one of his many victims would find him and kill him for what he did. Even if he is ever set free, he would never truly be free. If they let him out of *this* prison, he would just go to another prison without walls, guards, or protection. He would be a forty-five year old man sitting in front of a television for the rest of his life with no job, no money and no life. So, I guess he had chosen Greens so that he could live.

As for me, I chose life outside of Greens. I just wanted to be free. I wanted to make my own decisions. I didn't want the system for protection. I didn't need protection. I needed freedom and I hoped that Paul could make it happen.

It officially took six months for me to get my court date. The day before my court date seemed like it lasted forever. I was nervous all day. I was looking at everyone extra carefully all day. I didn't think they were going to let me walk out of there without at least one last attack.

I laid in my bed all night, restless. Uncle Don apologized all day for what he had done. I guess he was scared that I was going to kill him on my last night. He laid in the bunk under me, restless as well. I was thinking about tomorrow; he was just hoping that he would see tomorrow.

When my cell door started to open, we both sat up. Two guards walked into the room and looked at me.

"Jim, come with us."

"For what?"

"So they can kill you," Uncle Don said, jumping into the conversation. "You are finally going to get what you deserve, you sick son of a .." Just then, Anthony walked around the corner and into the cell. Don stopped talking and just stared at him.

"Let's go for a walk, we need to talk about some things."

I hopped out of bed and walked out of the cell. Anthony walked beside me as the guards followed about twenty feet behind us.

"What's up?"

"Son, this is one of your last nights here."

I interrupted, "You don't know that for sure."

He just looked at me and said, "Son, Paul don't lose, I told you that."

"Man, there is a first time for everything. With my luck, I will be the only case he will lose."

Anthony appeared frustrated and snapped, "Son, shut up."

Anthony knew, and I knew, that I was downplaying everything. I wasn't trying to get my hopes up because I couldn't take it if I lost again. I knew *Paul* could win, I just didn't know if it was in the cards for *me* to win. Sometimes it doesn't matter what you do, you are just meant to lose. I didn't know if this was one of those times that I was meant to lose.

Anthony and I kept walking and talking.

"Look, when you get on the outside, you can't do the same things you did in here. You're different now, but you have to kill that side of you. You have to keep in mind that you can be an animal when you are in a zoo, but once you leave the zoo you have to leave that animal behind."

"I hear you, but there is no way I am going to let what happened to me last time happen again."

"I am not saying be stupid and let someone invade you, all I am saying is just don't go on killing sprees. All that "get back" you did while you were in here, let it stay in here. Don't kill someone's mother because you see them spit in your hamburger from the drive-thru window."

I just looked at him and said, "You can't be serious. This is coming from the man who set people on fire for messing with his food."

Anthony couldn't help but laugh. "Alright, kill him, but leave his mother alone."

"Deal," I said, laughing also. After everything I had been through, I wished someone *would* spit in my food. I would deep-fry them, seriously.

Anthony continued, "You are protected in here, whether you believe it or not. If you would have killed three cops, they would have shot you on site, and investigated what happened later. In here, you are someone; out there, you are just another convict."

Anthony pulled out a cigarette and lit it. He took a couple of puffs and just looked around the dirty hallways.

"Started smoking for your health, I see."

Anthony just nodded as he inhaled again.

I appreciated everything he was saying, but the more he talked, the more I pitied him. He stayed in prison so that he could feel like someone, so he could feel like he was in control and empowered.

"Anthony, is this all you want? Come on, you have got to want more out of life than these walls."

Anthony looked away. He was hiding something.

"What's up man? What is it?"

"She is seventeen now. She just graduated high school and she is on her way to college," he said as he handed me a picture. "I was arrested for murder when I found out my girl was pregnant. When I found out, I decided not to even fight, but just to come here."

I stopped walking and asked, "What? You have a daughter and you are in here? You would rather stay in here than be with her?" That really upset me. I would have given anything to be with Crystal again and he had just given up his daughter like she was nothing.

Anthony jumped defensively and exclaimed, "You think I don't want to be with her? I can't. If my enemies found out about her, they would smoke her for sure."

"Screw them! Get out, take her and run. Hide out in the Midwest or something."

"Then she would be in prison and I can't do that to her," he said as he looked at the ground and puffed the cigarette.

My anger turned to sorrow. He wasn't even in jail to protect himself; he thought he had to stay in jail to protect his daughter. I wondered for a second if she even knew what was going through his head or if she just called him a no-good father and dropped it at that.

"Where is she?" I asked.

"Back in New York with her mother."

"Is that where you got the picture?"

"Yeah, she sends me things like this all the time. This picture was taken at her graduation. I wish I could have been there, but then again, she wouldn't want to see me."

"You don't know that. No matter what happened, you are her father. If she only knew the sacrifice that you are making for her," I paused. From his feelings, she could never know. She couldn't even know that he existed.

"Yeah. Well, that isn't going to happen."

We stood there for a second in silence. I felt really bad for him. The only way he felt he could show his daughter that he loved her was to never see her, but what kind of love was that?

"Why are you all the way down here?" I asked. I was curious how he made it from New York to here.

"I have done a lot of things."

I laughed a little bit and said, "I guess so."

He looked at me with a very serious face, "Do you believe in God?"

That question caught me off guard. Yeah, I believed in God, but I just hadn't thought about it for years now. I was too busy doing everything that I knew He wouldn't want me to do.

"Yeah, I believe in Him."

"Even after all of this, you believe that there is a God?"

"Yeah, I believe. What about you?"

"I guess, but sometimes it is hard. Son, look at all of the stuff that goes on. I mean, even in here, look at all of this. It is hard to imagine a God that would let all of this happen."

"This is our doing. Everything that happened in this world is because we did it. God doesn't let this stuff happen, He allows it to happen."

"What's the difference?" he asked while he finished off his cigarette and lit another one.

"To let it happen would imply that there was nothing He could do and He was powerless to stop it. To allow it to happen means that He could stop it at any time, but He just chooses not to."

"And you feel that is right?"

"Right or wrong, it's not up to me to decide. It is what it is."

Anthony took puff after puff as he leaned against the rail. "So, you think that everything happens for a reason?"

"There is always a reason."

"Then why are you here? If you really didn't kill Crystal, why are you here? What reason could there possibly be for you to be here right now?"

I stood there for a moment, stuck. I didn't know why I was there. I couldn't even think of a reason why I would be there. I knew I wasn't the best man to walk this earth, but I didn't think I did anything to deserve this. But then again, just because I didn't agree with Him didn't mean He was wrong.

"I really don't know the reason, but that doesn't mean there isn't one."

Anthony finished off his cigarette and said, "Well, let's get you back to your cell. You have a big day tomorrow."

We walked back down the hallway and back to my cell. Along the way, inmates were wishing me luck for the next day, which was now that day. It was funny, the first time I came here, everyone was ready for me to die. Now, everyone was pulling for me to live.

That night before I went to bed, I packed up all of my stuff. Just in case twelve people were crazy enough to let me out of here, I didn't want to have to come back for anything. I hoped and prayed that this was the last night I would have to spend in jail. I prayed that I would never have to see this place again. Who knew, maybe a prayer could get answered.

17

I was sitting in the courtroom next to Paul. Months earlier, he appeared before this judge to plea for my appeal. He told the judge that the State never proved their case; their whole case was, "If he didn't do it, then who did?" The judge agreed with Paul, but was not about to overrule the jury in that case, so he ordered another trial. This day, the trial started.

The State, in their stupidity, probably sent the weakest lawyer they had. Either they were very confident that they were not going to lose or they didn't have a lawyer with the heart to go against Paul.

The jury was selected and the trial started. The State's opening statement was long and drawn out. To sum it up, he said, "We already proved he was guilty."

When the State's lawyer finished, Paul leaned in to me, laughed and said, "Watch this." I thought it was funny when he said that. He said it the first time and pretty much won the case with his opening argument.

Paul stood up and walked to the jury. He looked at the jury of eight men and four women. He told me that he was trying to get emotion out of this case. Anyone led by emotion would convict me again because inside, they would feel that someone had to pay for Crystal's death, even if they didn't do it. I didn't necessarily agree with his way of thinking, but who am I? He knew what he was doing. He wasn't undefeated because he thought like the average man.

Paul looked mostly at the men during his opening statement. He occasionally glanced at the four females, only to acknowledge that they were there. He targeted the men, and he made it a point to make it known.

"Ladies and gentlemen of the jury, everything that I will say during this trial is going to be based on fact. Fact, Mr. Sutton would never hurt, let alone, kill his only daughter. Fact, the State has never proven that he killed Crystal. Fact, the State cannot prove that he was at the murder scene. Fact, the State doesn't even have a real motive as to why my client would want to kill his daughter."

He paused as he took a couple of steps back. "Ladies and gentlemen, all I want you to do is deal with the facts of this case. We all feel very bad that a five year old girl was abducted from her home and murdered; but no matter how bad you may feel, no one can feel any worse than Mr. Sutton. That was his daughter. That was his heart. That was his love."

He walked closer to the jury. "And that is the fact that everyone overlooked. That is the fact that everyone was missing. That is the fact that the State never looked at when they accused my client, gave him the worst representation possible for the first trial and sent him off to jail to die. You, ladies and gentlemen, cannot forget that facts."

He walked back over to our table and sat down. The judge asked the State to call their first witness. The attorney was so stuck on Paul's opening statement that he just sat there for a minute, completely ignoring the judge.

The judge asked the State to call its first witness again, this time shouting at him. He jumped up, pulled himself from his daze and called the head detective on my case, Detective Chambers.

Detective Chambers walked up to the stand, was sworn in and sat down. The State's attorney walked up and started to ask him questions.

"Mr. Chambers, please state your profession for the court."

"I am a Detective for the Scottsdale Police Department."

"And were you the head detective of the case involving the murder of Crystal Sutton?"

"Yes, I was."

"Did you charge Jim Sutton with the murder of Crystal Sutton?"

"Yes, I did."

"What made you come to the conclusion that Mr. Sutton murdered his daughter?"

"He had the means to kill her. He was the last one to have seen her alive. He had the motive to kill her. We investigated this case thoroughly and used every available resource. We searched his home and found no forced entry. There is no one with a key besides Mr. and Mrs. Sutton."

"And did you question Mrs. Sutton about her whereabouts?"

"Yes, I did."

"And?"

"She was at work at the time of the disappearance. She couldn't come home because she didn't even have a car. Mr. Sutton dropped her off at work."

"Was there any other reason that brought you to the decision that Mr. Sutton killed his daughter?"

"Yes, there was a fight in the house that morning."

"Fight? How do you know?"

"We questioned the neighbors. His next door neighbor informed us that there was a big commotion that morning in the house. She stated that it sounded like a big fight was going on."

"And what did Mr. Sutton say about this so-called fight?"

"Nothing. He just said that there was no fight; but he couldn't even look at me after I mentioned the fight," he said as he turned and looked at the jury.

"Was there any evidence to suggest that he was at the scene?"

"Yes, we found a shoe print that matched the exact shoe size of Mr. Sutton."

"So, if I am hearing this correctly Detective Chambers, you used 'facts' to charge Mr. Sutton."

"Yes, sir, we used nothing but facts to charge and convict Mr. Sutton."

Paul turned to me as his faced turned blood red. He whispered to me, "They have officially pissed me off."

The judge stated that Paul may cross-examine.

Paul stood up and went to work on Detective Chambers. He walked over to the witness stand and stood directly in front of him.

"Mr. Chambers, I would like to go over some of the testimony that you have given today and would like to touch on some of the testimony you gave in the previous trial."

"Okay."

"Mr. Chambers, let me first ask, what did you mean by 'he had the means to kill her'?"

"I meant that he was with her in the house. He was stronger than her. He could easily have killed her."

"Okay, and you said that you had the motive. What was the motive that you came up with?"

"Well, we felt that there could have been an argument that morning that caused all of this to start. Mr. Sutton stressed to us that he was very big on respect, and it is possible that she did something he felt was disrespectful."

Paul smiled, "Mr. Chambers, you just testified that he had a motive to kill her."

"Yes, I did."

"Well, what was the motive?"

"Unfortunately, I do not know for sure."

"I guess that wasn't part of the investigation."

The State's attorney was about to object, but Chambers started talking.

"I apologize that I do not know why someone would kill their daughter. I am sorry, Mr. Reed, but there are a lot of sick people out here that do things for reasons even I can't explain."

"Mr. Chambers, I respect your honesty, but I am sure the jury would have loved to hear the truth. The fact of the matter is you have no idea what reason Mr. Sutton would have had to kill Crystal."

"No, sir, I don't."

"Okay, you just testified that you investigated this case thoroughly and used every possible resource. Is that correct?"

"Yes, sir, we did."

"Did you check with Mrs. Sutton's employer to see if she left during that day?"

"No, sir, we didn't."

"Did you check with her co-workers to see if she went missing for an extended period of time?"

"No sir, we didn't."

"You said that she couldn't even come home. But in the police report, the officer on the scene said that Mr. Sutton called her at work and she arrived at the house about fifteen to twenty minutes later. Is that correct?"

"Yes, sir."

"Well, how did she get home?"

"I guess a co-worker drove her home."

"You guess? You said that this was a thorough investigation. Is guessing included in a thorough investigation?"

"Objection," said the States attorney.

"Overruled," said the judge. He looked at the Detective and said, "Please answer the question."

"Every investigation includes some guess work. This investigation was no different."

"You searched the house, correct?"

"Yes, officers on the scene searched the house and after the arrest was made, we searched the house again."

"Did they find anything that suggested a fight or altercation had taken place?"

"I don't believe so."

"Did they find any blood or weapons laying around the house?"

"I do not believe they did."

"Did you check the house for blood or any weapons that could have been used?"

"The first time I do not believe they did; the second time we *did* check for blood and weapons."

"Did you find any?"

"No, we didn't; but we believed that Mr. Sutton attempted to cover up any sign of a fight or struggle and could have hidden any evidence."

"Yes, the fight," Paul said, walking back to the table and grabbing his notepad. "You said that you talked to the neighbors and they said that there was a big commotion going on in the house. That statement led you to believe that there was a fight in the house, correct?"

"Yes."

"Did they ever hear commotion from the house before?"

"One witness said that she would hear commotion all of the time. She thought that he was very abusive because she would hear banging and noises just about every morning. She didn't know what was going on, but she said that it concerned her."

"So, this morning was no different then? If she heard noises every morning, what made that day special?"

"Crystal was killed that day."

"Right….right, and you believed this fight that you have no evidence of, was the cause of her death."

"We believe that is where it all started from."

"And where do you believe it ended?"

"With her getting choked to death and set on fire."

Some members of the jury let out a sigh.

"Where did she die?" Paul asked.

"We believe that she died in the house," Mr. Chambers replied.

"Do you have any physical evidence to suggest that she died in the house?"

"No, we believe Mr. Sutton removed all of the evidence from the house."

Paul smiled at the jury and looked back at the witness, "Mr. Chambers, let me make sure that I am hearing you correctly. To everything that I have asked, most of your answers included, 'I believe, we believe, or could have.' Is that the evidence that was used in making your decision to go after my client?"

"We believed that he was a suspect and when all of the evidence pointed to him, we decided to charge him with murder."

"What evidence? All you have told this court and this jury was what you believed. You have told us your opinion. You have yet to provide ANY evidence whatsoever."

"Mr. Reed, our investigation was extremely thorough. He was convicted of murder because of the evidence that was brought forth in the first trial."

"Yes, the evidence. Let's go on the only physical evidence that you have.

You said that you found a footprint at the crime scene. You also said that the footprint was the same size as Mr. Sutton's, correct?"

"Yes, sir, it was the exact size."

"Exact size, got it. Did the footprint have treads in it?"

"Yes, it did."

"Did you match the treads in the shoe to any shoe that my client owned?"

"No. Mr. Sutton did not have a shoe matching the shoe that made the footprint."

"Then how can you positively say my client was there?"

"We believe that Mr. Sutton got rid of all of the physical evidence, including the shoes that made the print."

"Mr. Chambers, did you ask Mrs. Sutton if he owned a pair of shoes like the ones that made the footprint?"

"No, I didn't."

Paul just shook his head from side to side and asked, "Mr. Chambers, is it safe for this court to assume that your entire case was based around opinion and not fact?"

"No, we have physical evidence, Mr. Reed."

"Physical evidence that you can't prove belongs to my client."

Detective Chambers just sat there and didn't say anything. Paul dismissed him and sat down beside me.

"That was too easy," he said as he grabbed a cup and poured some water.

Detective Chambers was one of the main reasons that they convicted me last time. Scott was the other reason. With Paul as my lawyer and Detective Chambers' whole investigation ripped apart, the State didn't have much left.

They brought in other witnesses to talk about Crystal's death. They tried to do the same thing they did last time, but the only problem for them was that I had Paul this time. He pushed for physical evidence and facts. He had a jury made mostly of men who he believed would look more for facts and wouldn't say guilty off of sheer emotion.

Once the State had called all of their witnesses, Paul closed the deal. He stood up and approached the judge.

"Your honor, the burden of proof was placed on the prosecution and they have yet to answer that burden. From their witnesses' own mouths, they have revealed that their whole case is based solely on opinion, not fact. Their whole case was based on belief, not evidence; and I request that the case be thrown out on the grounds of lack of evidence."

The judge looked at Paul long and hard. He then turned to the State's attorney and asked, "Do you have anything that you would like to say?"

"No, your honor. We feel that we have proven our case and shown that Mr. Sutton is guilty without a shadow of a doubt."

"Well, Mr. Reed seems to think that you haven't proven anything," the judge stated.

"With all due respect, your honor, his opinion means nothing to me," the State's attorney said, turning and looking at Paul like he was nothing.

"Well, I agree with his opinion. And since it seems that this entire case is based on opinion, I will give you mine. The next time you come into my courtroom, you might want to try to make sure an investigation was actually done," he said, looking at the attorney and then looking at Detective Chambers.

"You have taken five years of this man's life based on the opinion of a Detective. You had no physical evidence then, and you have none now. You had no motive and still don't. You don't even know where the place of death was. Was an autopsy done on the body?"

The attorney turned around and looked at Chambers. He shook his head no. The attorney looked back at the judge and answered, "No, your honor."

The judge looked down at some papers in a folder. "In the last trial, the body was identified as Crystal Sutton. How was the body identified?"

"Through dental records, your honor."

"So, at least you got the right body," he said, shaking his head in disbelief.

"Yes, your honor."

"Great, now all you have to do is find the person who killed her. And if you happen to find that person, please obtain the evidence that can prove that he or she was the person who committed the crime."

The judge turned, looked at me and said, "Mr. Sutton, on behalf of the State, I would like to be the first person to apologize to you for all that you have gone through. The State failed to prove its case; but worse, the State failed to provide you with adequate representation, and for that I apologize. The system failed you, Mr. Sutton, but not any longer. This case has been dismissed because of lack of evidence against the defendant."

My heart raced with excitement.

"Mr. Sutton, you are free to go."

I looked at the judge like he was crazy. I looked at Paul, not really knowing what to do next.

Paul looked up at the judge and said, "Thank you, your honor."

Paul turned to me with the biggest smile on his face and said, "You are free. You are a free man."

Then it hit me. I was free. I was free. I jumped up and down for a second, then I grabbed Paul and hugged him.

"Thank you! Thank you so much!" I exclaimed.

18

Paul grabbed his stuff and said, "Let's go. Let's get you out of here before they change their minds."

I knew he was joking, but I wasn't about to take the chance. As the judge was dismissing the jury, Paul and I escaped out of the door. We walked down the hallway and out of the front door. I held my composure as long as I could, but as soon as we hit the front door and I was outside, I screamed like a mad man. "YESSSSSSSSSSSSSS!!! I can't believe it! I CAN'T BELIEVE IT!!! I am free!" I put my hands over my mouth so that I could scream even louder, "I'M FREE!!!"

Paul looked at me and just smiled. "Yes, you are free. Here, this is for you," he said as he handed me an envelope. I opened the envelope and pulled out a letter and some money.

"Paul, you have done so much for me. I couldn't possibly take this from you," I said, handing the envelope back to him.

Paul laughed and replied, "Don't worry, it's not from me. Besides, you owe me too much money for me to give you anything." He pushed my hand with the envelope back towards me. "It is five thousand - one for every year. Spend it wisely or blow it. I don't care, it is your money."

I started to flip through the money. I never had that much money at one time in my life. All of this just seemed surreal. It felt like I was dreaming.

Paul pulled his keys out of his pocket and asked, "Do you have a place to stay?"

"No, I didn't even think I was getting out."

"Do you want to call someone, your parents perhaps?" Paul asked, as he handed me his cell phone.

"No, my parents died about eight years ago and I don't know of anyone else to call."

"Okay, let's go."

Paul walked me to his car, which was a 2012 Mercedes Benz. They just finished pushing out the 2011 model and he already had next year's model. We got into the car and he drove me to a nice hotel on the west side of Pineville, which was about thirty miles away from Scottsdale. On the way to the hotel, his cell phone rang. He answered it and told whoever was on the other end to meet him at the hotel. When we arrived at the hotel, we got out of the car and walked inside. I pulled out my money to pay for the room. When the man finally got to us, Paul asked for the manager. The manager walked up and as soon as he saw, Paul he started laughing.

"Hello my friend," the manager said with a heavy foreign accent.

"Hello, Pedro. How are you?"

"Fine, fine. What do you need today?"

"I need a room for my friend," Paul said as he patted me on my shoulder.

"Is that all? Here, he can have the suite on the top floor. Beautiful view, overlook the city, he like."

He handed Paul the keycard and Paul handed it to me. We walked to the elevator, went to the top floor and walked to the room. Paul told me to go in and get comfortable. He would be right back.

I walked into the room. It was huge! It was like an apartment. There was a sitting area that looked more like a living room. They had a big screen television in the sitting area and a nice size television in the bedroom. The bathroom had a stand-up shower and a Jacuzzi tub. There were three mini refrigerators loaded with food and drinks throughout the suite. The bedroom looked like it took up the entire top floor and the bed had to be the size of two queen size beds.

I had walked around the suite about four times before Paul knocked on the door. I ran to open the door and let him in. Paul walked in, but not alone. Another man who was a little bit taller than Paul walked in behind him. He walked directly past me and into the sitting area. He placed the bag that he was carrying on the chair, opened it up, and started to remove some kind of equipment.

I looked at Paul, confused. "Is everything okay?"

Paul looked at me and ordered, "Just close the door and come on over here."

I closed the door and walked over to the sitting area. I sat down on the sofa and watched both of them closely. Paul and the gentleman were pulling things out of the bag. The gentleman started to put a camera together as Paul went around adjusting the light in the room. He took the lampshades off the lamps and even brought in extra light from the bedroom.

Once they had everything set up, Paul looked at me and said, "Remember when I said later… well, it's later."

I started to get nervous. If this man's idea of payment was to have sex with me while filming it, he was crazy. I knew that I hadn't been out of jail for even two hours yet, but I was about to go back if that was his plan.

"Come on. We need you to stand up and take off your shirt."

That was it. Both of these men were about to be on the ten o'clock news.

Paul saw the expression on my face and must have known what I was thinking. He quickly commented. "Oh man, where is my brain? I am sorry Jim. This is Jeff. He is the photographer that I hired. He is going to help me with your case."

I was still very defensive and my facial expression did not change as I asked, "What case? I thought my case was over?"

Paul smiled and replied, "I'm talking about the wrongful imprisonment lawsuit that we are going to file against the State. I have a number in my head, Jim. Can you guess the number that I am thinking?"

"I'm sorry, I don't know," I said, slowly calming down and releasing some of the anger that just built up. I had to laugh to myself as I thought, *the cup was full Paul, the cup was full.*

Paul, seeing that I was calming down, continued his little game, "Come on, just throw a number out there."

"Twenty."

"Higher," he said, holding his thumb up.

"Thirty-five."

"Higher," he said, still holding his thumb up to the ceiling.

"Fifty."

Paul winked at me.

"Fifty thousand, that is not bad. What do you get, like forty of it?"

Paul laughed at me. Even Jeff, the camera man, laughed.

"Well, I can't argue. If you want the whole fifty, I won't be mad. It is money well deserved."

Paul looked at me like I was clueless and said, "Fifty million, not fifty thousand."

Fifty million! Fifty million! My brain couldn't even process the possibility of getting fifty million dollars.

"We are going to sue for one hundred million, but the most we will get is fifty."

Paul had a really bad habit of saying things that left my brain paralyzed.

"Fifty million, you are going to sue the State for fifty million...dollars," I said, struggling to get the words out.

"No Jim, we are going to sue the State for a hundred million, but we will get fifty," Paul said with confidence.

"And you are going to win?"

Paul looked at me like I was still clueless and responded, "I do not lose, Jim. Yes, WE are going to win."

I was speechless. That is what he meant by 'later'.

"So, what do you need me to do?"

"I need you to get undressed so Jeff can take pictures of the wounds you sustained while you were incarcerated. This is going to be one of the first things that we are going to present to the jury."

"And I take it that your jury is going to be made up of all women," I asked while I pulled off my shirt.

Paul winked at me again and asked, "You are catching on quick, aren't you?"

I removed my shirt and threw it on the chair. Jeff looked upon me in horror. His face was blood red as he grabbed his stomach with both of his hands. He couldn't take the sight. He ran into the bathroom and vomited everything that was in his stomach into the toilet. When his stomach was empty, I could hear him gagging up air. His body was still throwing up even though there was nothing left.

Paul looked upon me with sorrow and amazement. He walked over to me and just stared at every stitch, every wound, every scar repeatedly.

"My God, how are you still alive?"

I laughed and answered, "Your guess is as good as mine. They couldn't kill me. I guess someone was praying for me."

Paul just stared at my body. He asked, "Does it still hurt?"

"No, but some of the wounds still bleed from time to time."

Paul pulled his cell phone out of his coat pocket. He flipped it open, hit a couple of buttons, and put the phone to his ear.

"Hey, it's me. I need you at the hotel in ten minutes," he said into the phone. He walked around me and looked at my back. The sight of my back made him drop his phone. He scrambled to pick it back up and added, "Make it five."

He hung up his phone and continued to examine me. Jeff was still in the bathroom throwing up nothing, but still throwing up.

I turned to Paul and asked, "Is he going to be okay?"

Paul was still in a daze as he stared at my back. I don't think he even heard me.

"How in the world are you alive? You are like Frankenstein. You have stitches everywhere," he said, talking more to himself than to me.

"Paul!" I shouted, trying to get his attention.

He jumped. "Yes," he said, startled.

"Is Jeff going to be okay?"

"Jeff" he said, looking confused. Just then Jeff gagged again into the toilet. "Jeff!" he shouted, realizing he was in the bathroom, dying.

Paul started to walk towards the bathroom when he heard a knock at the door. He turned from the bathroom and walked towards the door. When he opened the door, a man walked in holding what appeared to be a physician's bag.

"Hey Paul."

"You are late. What took you so long?" Paul asked, with a little bit of anger in his voice.

"I am sorry, I was eating when you called me. What in the world is so important? I was enjoying the most delicious ribs on this planet."

Paul closed the door and walked him over to me.

"Jim, this is Dr. Bowman. Dr. Bowman, this is Jim. He's the guy I was telling you about a couple of weeks ago."

The doctor reached his hand out to shake mine and said, "Nice to meet you."

I shook his hand and replied, "Nice to meet you, too."

Jeff gagged again in the bathroom, but I don't think Paul even noticed.

Dr. Bowman turned to Paul and asked, "Is he okay?"

Paul, realizing that he forgot about Jeff again, turned and ran into the bathroom.

"Okay, let's see what we have here," Dr. Bowman said, opening up his bag. He started to examine my chest and stomach. His face started to turn different colors as well. Paul sure got a good room for the situation. If we only had one bathroom, the maintenance crew was going to be in trouble.

Dr. Bowman looked up at me with utter confusion on his face and asked, "How are you still alive?"

Paul came running out of the bathroom and chimed in, "That is what I said."

Dr. Bowman ran his fingers over several of my wounds. "These are not even closed properly. Do they bleed from time to time?"

"Yes, about three to four times a week."

Dr. Bowman shook his head and stated, "Green's doctors are worthless."

I understood what he was saying, but I had to disagree. "Not worthless, they just don't care.

"If you are a doctor and don't care, then you are worthless."

Okay, he won. They were worthless.

He looked at Paul and asked, "How much time do I have?"

"Why?" Paul asked.

"Because he needs to have ninety percent of these wounds cut open and stitched together correctly. They are never going to heal like this and they are also prone to infection. If he brushes against the wrong handrail with open wounds like these, he could be dead in six months."

"If you do it now, how long would it take for him to heal?"

"If he does nothing but rest, he should be okay in two months."

Paul looked at me and asked, "Is that okay with you?"

"I really don't have anywhere to go or anything to do. I have nothing but time."

Paul looked at Dr. Bowman and said, "Do it."

"I am sorry, one question," I said as Dr. Bowman pulled out his cell phone. "How much is this going to cost?"

Dr. Bowman paid me no attention and opened up his phone. He called his office and told them to prepare for emergency surgery at the Surgery Center.

Paul walked over to me and suggested, "Let's go outside."

We walked out to the balcony that overlooked the city. Paul shut the balcony door and sat down on the patio chair.

"Jim, why do you keep asking about money?"

"I really don't mean to burden you, but I really don't have anything right now. I really appreciate all that you have done for me and all that you are still doing, but I don't want anything to go wrong and then you look at me for payment. I know that you don't lose, but in the event that lightning does strike, I wouldn't have anything to give you."

Paul understood where I was coming from. He told me to sit down beside him.

"Jim, I know you don't have anything. I haven't asked you for anything. You really don't understand who I am and what I do? For whatever reason, Anthony brought you to me; and because he brought you to me, it is now my responsibility to take care of you. The lawsuit against the State is for you, to set you up for life." He paused for a second. "Jim, I don't need money. If I did, do you think that you would have gotten the five thousand dollars? Do you think money is a concern when I have a doctor on call or when I get the most expensive hotel room in the most expensive hotel in the city for six months?"

I looked at him shocked and questioned incredulously, "Six months?"

"Yeah, do you have somewhere else to go?"

I shook my head no.

"So stop worrying, I got this."

"Yes, sir."

Paul got up to go back into the room.

"One more thing," I said. Paul stopped and turned around. If he was getting frustrated, he did an excellent job of hiding it. "If Jeff dies in the bathroom, what are we going to do with the body? I just came from court and I really don't feel like going back."

Paul's eyes got wide. He opened the door and ran back into the bathroom. Jeff was sitting on the floor, trying to catch his breath.

I walked back into the room, closed the balcony door and walked up to Dr. Bowman.

"You have surgery scheduled at six o'clock. Get everything you need to bring with you and let's go."

"What about Jeff?" I asked, genuinely concerned about him. He came here to help me, but the sight of me got the best of him and his stomach.

Dr. Bowman looked into his bag and said, "Paul, give him this medicine for the nausea."

"He can't hold anything down!" Paul yelled from the bathroom.

"I know. This medicine is not to be taken orally."

Paul walked out of the bathroom, "He is a dead man if you think I am going to stick that up his...."

Dr. Bowman interjected, "Never mind, I will do it."

Dr. Bowman searched through his bag for a second and pulled out a pair of rubber gloves. He closed up his bag, slapped on the gloves and went into the bathroom with the medicine in hand.

Paul and I both looked at each other. "Couldn't be me," I said.

Paul just laughed and added, "Couldn't be me either."

Dr. Bowman came out of the bathroom just as the fax machine in the room started to ring. Dr. Bowman was drying his hands off as he walked over to the fax machine and grabbed some of the pages that came through. He started to read the fax. The more he read, the more he shook his head in disbelief.

"How are you alive?" he asked as he looked up from the fax.

That was the third time I had been asked that question, but I still didn't know how to answer it. I just shrugged my shoulders and replied, "I have no idea."

Paul walked over to him and looked at the fax.

"You were in the infirmary thirty-seven times? What in the world was going on in there?" Paul asked.

I looked at Paul and gave him the only answer that came to mind. "War. They wanted me dead and they took their shots for about two and a half years."

Dr. Bowman jumped in, "You were in Greens for about five and a half years. You were incarcerated from January of 2006 to July 14, 2011." He flipped through the pages as Paul grabbed the rest of the fax off the machine.

"Five and a half years?" I asked. I thought it was only five.

"Yeah, they counted the time you served before you went to trial," Dr. Bowman said.

"Oh, I had forgotten about those six months. I just counted from the time that I was convicted. I didn't know those days counted."

Paul and Dr. Bowman continued to read the fax. They both must have read something at the same time, because both of them stopped reading at the same time and looked at me.

"You were officially dead twice," Dr. Bowman said. "One time for six minutes and one time for four minutes."

"When?" I asked.

"You died for six minutes on August 12, 2006 and for four minutes on November 6, 2007. This fax says that you died during the night both times."

"Well, at least they saved me."

Paul laughed and stated, "They don't save inmates at Greens, you should know that."

Now the question that everyone was asking, I started to ask myself, "*How was I alive?*"

19

Once Dr. Bowman finished reviewing my medical records from Greens, we all made our way to the Surgery Center of Pineville. When we arrived, I was rushed into the building and prepped for surgery. The surgery itself lasted seven hours. He had to cut open and properly stitch up over fifty wounds, ranging from my neck all the way to my lower thigh.

At first he didn't want to do it because he was scared I wouldn't make it through; but I assured him that after everything I had been through, this surgery would be nothing. The surgery was successful. He said that I should be up and running in about two months, as long as I didn't do anything to pop the stitches.

Paul took me back to the hotel around two o'clock in the morning. I hadn't eaten anything since breakfast at the courthouse, and that was nothing but a bagel. Paul ran out to a convenient store and picked up roughly four bags of food. It was mostly junk food like cookies, chips and soda. He did manage to find some food though. He got me some of those microwavable cheeseburgers and subs the convenience stores sell.

I thanked Paul for everything, ate a couple of sandwiches and bags of chips and went to bed.

Even though I had the most comfortable bed imaginable, I couldn't sleep. The stitches on my back were killing me. I had fresh stitches on my arms and shoulders that made sleeping on my side impossible; and my chest was like a jigsaw puzzle, so that was out. I knew Dr. Bowman said the stitches would dissolve by themselves in a few weeks, but I was seriously contemplating removing a few myself just so I could go to sleep.

I got up and walked into the sitting room. I turned on the television to see if there was anything on.

I had already taken the pain medication that Dr. Bowman gave me, but it hadn't kicked in yet. He said it was going to make me drowsy, but I wasn't feeling it.

I flipped through channel after channel on the television, but there was nothing on. It was summertime, so even the sports scene was pretty much dead.

I turned the television off, got up and walked out on the balcony. The manager was right, the view was beautiful. All I could see were lights, as far as my eyes could see. There were a few cars driving the streets, but other than that, it was empty. It looked so peaceful, so quiet and so calm.

I sat on a patio chair as I gazed out upon the city. Before long, my medicine started to kick in and I didn't even feel the pain from the stitches pulling and holding my skin together. I just sat there, relaxed and happy. I soon dozed off in the chair. My first night out of prison was spent outside in the cool summer's breeze, and I loved it.

The next morning, I woke up just as the sun was rising. I stretched my arms and back as I got up out of the chair. My body was very sore. I guess the medicine had worn off during the night.

I walked to the end of the balcony to get a better view of the city when I heard yelling coming from the room. It stunned me because nobody should have been in the room, especially in the room yelling.

I opened the balcony door and slowly walked into the room. Before I could close the door, a man ran out from the bathroom. He was a skinny, short man, shorter than Paul, and I could see his ribs through his shirt. He stood there for a moment like a deer staring at an oncoming car.

Before I could even open my mouth, he shouted, "Paul, I think I found him!"

Paul came rushing out of the bedroom. "Where were you at?" Paul asked frantically.

"I was outside on the balcony," I said as I closed the door.

"Did you fall asleep out there?"

"I must have," I said. I attempted to sit down on the chair without causing further pain to my stitches.

"Did you take your medicine yet?" Paul asked, concerned.

"No, I'm sorry, I just woke up."

Paul went into the bathroom to get my medicine. "It says you have to take it with food!" he shouted from the bathroom.

The man Paul brought with him was still standing there, looking at me. I had my shirt off. The stitches by themselves were painful, but to have cotton rubbing against them repeatedly was unbearable. He was stuck looking at the scars and wounds all over my body. I thought we were going to have another Jeff episode.

"Paul, you might want to help your friend."

Paul ran out of the bathroom and saw him just standing there. Paul laughed at him for a second, then snapped his fingers in front of his face.

"Hello, Earth to Greg."

Greg jumped as his mind came back to his body.

"Greg, are you going to be okay?" I asked.

"Yeah, yeah, I will be fine," he responded, still staring at me.

"Would you like for me to put on a shirt?"

Greg looked down to the ground, trying to stop staring and said, "No, no, you are fine."

Paul jumped in, "No, you can't. Greg is here to take the pictures, but from the looks of it, we are going to need to call Dr. Bowman again," he said, laughing out loud at his own joke. "Greg....Greg, set the camera up."

Greg ran to the bag where the camera was located. He pulled out all of the equipment and set up the camera. Paul went around closing all of the curtains and adjusting the lights in the room.

When everything was ready, they started to take pictures of my wounds. They photographed everything: bruises, cuts, stabs, the mark the beanbag left, everything. It took about four hours and five rolls of film before Paul was satisfied.

After he was done, Paul went to get some food from a Chinese restaurant. We sat around and ate, ate real well. I liked hanging around Paul. He had money, but he wasn't cheap; and he didn't mind helping others.

Around three o'clock, Paul and Greg left. Paul told me that he was going to the courthouse to file the lawsuit and he had to drop Greg off to have the film developed. Paul was going to push for a trial as soon as possible. With the people Paul knew and the strings that he could pull, I knew it wasn't going to be long.

For the rest of the week I pretty much rested. I spent most of my time eating, watching the city go by during the day, watching the sun set, then watching the city light up at night. My personal favorite was the sunset. It was absolutely beautiful. I would look at the people in the streets walk past the hotel everyday and wonder how no one would stop to marvel at such a beautiful site. I figured they took it for granted. People really don't know what they have until they don't have it anymore.

20

After sitting in the hotel room for a week, boredom finally paid me a visit. At first, I would just eat a little more or watch television, but the boredom wouldn't leave. I decided to get out of the room, just for a day.

I looked up Maria. I found her name in the phone book and decided to catch the bus and go see her. She was still in Scottsdale, living in one of those upscale apartments on the east side of town.

She wasn't home when I arrived, but one of her neighbors told me that she was down at the police station. I got on another bus and went down to the Scottsdale Police Station. I really didn't want to go inside. The last time I went inside of this building, I came out in handcuffs with life in prison staring me in the face. So, needless to say, I wasn't exactly thrilled to be walking back into it.

I sucked it up and opened the door. I walked to the front desk and asked to speak to Detective Diaz. The young cop sitting behind the counter jumped to his feet and ran to tell her that she had a visitor. He came back moments later and said that she would see me as he pointed to the office in the back.

I walked through the rows of desks and straight to the back office. I knocked on the door before I opened it.

"Come on in," she said.

When I walked into the room, her mouth dropped opened. She looked angry and shocked all at the same time.

"What are you doing here?" she asked, from her desk.

"I came here to see you. I am out!"

"Obviously," she observed coldheartedly.

"Did I come at a bad time?"

"No, I just don't know what you are doing here. I am curious as to what you want?"

"I just wanted to see you. You visited me a lot in prison and you were the only person that I really wanted to see when I got out."

Maria got up, walked over to the door and shut it.

"Did you ever think about why I stopped coming to see you?"

I did think about that, a lot. I knew that she had stopped coming because of the laundry room incident, but I really wasn't trying to bring that up again.

"I figured you got tired of me," I said, just trying to say something to answer her question.

"Don't play with me. You know why I stopped coming to see you and why I stopped dealing with you. Don't stand here and pretend like you are dumb," she said, still holding the doorknob in her hand.

"Maria, what do you want me to say? I am trying to put that part of my life behind me. I have a fresh start now. I am not trying to re-live that stuff," I said. I sat down in the chair in front of her desk.

Maria let go of the door and walked back to her desk. She sat down and leaned in towards me. "The officers that were killed, do they get a fresh start? The wives of those officers, do they get a fresh start? The children of those officers, where is their fresh start? You may want to put it in the rearview mirror, but they can't. They are still living with what you did everyday. Don't you dare talk to me about moving on with your life, because you are the only one who can move on. Everyone else is stuck with that day forever."

I allowed a little bit of time to pass before I talked, hoping that she would calm down a little.

"First of all, they were trying to kill me, but I guess that doesn't matter."

She interrupted me, "You don't know that for sure."

I noticed she didn't calm down, but I was out of patience waiting for her to. I stood up and pulled off my shirt. The pain of the cotton running along the stitches brought tears to my eyes, and I couldn't take the medication because it made me sleepy. She stared at me for a minute and her eyes watered up.

"They tried to kill me for three years. So when they pulled me out of my cell that night, I was not thinking about their wives or their children. I was thinking that if one of those guards were to hit me, I would show no mercy; and I didn't."

Maria sat there trying to show as little emotion as possible, but still crying. She protested, "That doesn't make it right. Those scars do not justify what you did. Those scars do not give you the right to do whatever you want to do."

"No, I need a badge for that," I replied. I was upset. The more she talked, the angrier I became.

The comment had struck a nerve inside of her and she demanded, "What is that supposed to mean?"

"You know what it means. That faggot Chambers had me convicted because of his opinion, because he guessed about what happened."

Maria took great offense to that and stated, "Detective Chambers is a very good police officer, despite what you and your despicable lawyer may think."

I jumped in, "Don't forget about the judge."

Maria rolled her eyes and said, "I don't care what was said in that courtroom. I -"

I cut her off, "That's apparent, or you would have showed up." It really did irk me that she hadn't come to the trial. I thought that no matter what happened, she would always support me. I thought we had grown close. I guess I overestimated her affection for me.

"What did I have to show up for? There was nothing there for me."

I looked at her with my blood boiling inside and questioned, "Nothing? So I am nothing now?"

"You know what I mean," she said.

"Obviously I don't. I must have missed something."

Maria stood up from her chair and exclaimed, "Don't try and turn this on me! We are talking about you and what you did."

I stood up and asked, "What did I do? Tell me what I did wrong."

She walked from around her desk and over to me. "You killed three officers. You murdered them and didn't even think twice about it," she said. She tried to whisper, but the anger in her voice still made it come out loud.

"Look at me," I said calmly. "Do you think they would have thought twice?"

"That doesn't matter."

"What?" I exploded, "Why doesn't that matter? You mean to say that if they killed me it would have been okay; but because I killed them, I am wrong?"

"That is not what I am saying."

"Then what *are* you saying? All I am hearing is how wrong I am for being alive."

Maria blurted out, "You are better than that! Or at least, I thought you were. They were animals, but I expected you to be above that. I expected you to act better than they acted. I expected you to act human."

"I am sorry, but they killed the human inside of me. They wanted a beast and that is exactly what they got - a beast."

"I know you are not trying to justify yourself by saying it's their fault."

"I don't have to justify myself at all, every mark, every bruise, every cut and every stitch does it for me."

Maria looked at my chest. Then she walked around me and looked at my back. When she walked back in front of me, tears were collecting on her chin. She walked to her desk and grabbed some tissue from a Kleenex box. After she wiped her face, she sat down.

"Jim, what happened to you? What happened to the man who cried in prison because he missed Crystal so much? What happened to the man who called me everyday when she was missing? What happened to the man that loved first and hated last? What happened to that man?"

I looked at her with sorrow in my eyes but coldness in my heart and said, "I am sorry, Maria, but they killed him in prison. He died on August 12, 2006 and again on November 6, 2007."

She looked down and said, "I guess so."

I put my shirt back on and walked out of her office. I walked back to the bus stop to wait for the bus. I thought about the conversation that Maria and I had all the way back to the hotel. I wished that it had turned out differently, turned out better; but I had to tell the truth. The human part of me did die. They couldn't save it, they only saved the beast.

21

I arrived back at the hotel after a long bus ride. I kept playing the conversation with Maria over and over again in my brain. I hated feeling like I should have said something more. I shouldn't have let the conversation end that way. She was all that I had left in my life, and I might have just lost her.

When I got off the elevator, the conversation I had with Anthony popped into my head. I remembered him telling me, "You have to kill that side of you. You have to leave the animal in the zoo." *Easier said than done*, I thought to myself.

I opened the door to the hotel room and walked in. I threw the keycard on a little table that was by the door. As soon as the door closed, Paul came from around the corner with a sandwich in his hand.

"These sandwiches are terrible," he said, taking another bite.

"Try prison food," I said as I laughed.

Paul took another bite and asked, "Where have you been?"

"I just had to get out of here for awhile and get some fresh air," I said, walking to the living room to sit down. "What have you been up to? I haven't seen you in a week."

"I have been busy keeping you out of jail," Paul said, taking another bite.

"What do you mean keeping me out of jail? And by the way, if that sandwich is so bad, why are you still eating it?" I asked.

"You have received restraining orders from over fifteen different people. To the second question, I am hungry. Do you have any more?" Paul asked as he took another bite.

"Restraining orders for what? And there are more sandwiches in the fridge. Do you want some chips?"

"For the people you threatened. Where are the chips?" Paul asked as he looked in the refrigerator for another sandwich.

"Paul, talk to me for one second. I know that you are hungry, but what people are we talking about here?"

Paul stood up from the refrigerator.

"The people that were writing you while you were in prison. You know the letters you received from people that cursed you and wanted you dead? Well, as soon as they heard you were out of prison, they all ran to their lawyers and to their courts to file papers that prohibit you from coming within a hundred feet of them."

I had no choice but to laugh as I said, "Okay, these people write letters stating that they want to kill me, and now they are looking for protection."

"Pretty much," Paul said, taking another bite. "They are all scared for their lives. One guy even sold his house and had his name changed."

"I hope you took care of those for me."

"All except one," Paul said, popping open a bag of chips. "You can't go to Alaska for a while."

"That is too funny," I said. "Everyone was all big and bad while I was locked up. Now that I am out, everyone is scared! That is what they get. I hope they live in fear for the rest of their lives. Stupid mother......."

Paul stopped me, "Don't worry about them. They are pointless."

"But come on Paul, they mailed me letter after letter saying what they wanted to do to me and what they wished happened. I should kill them off of principal."

Paul put his hands over his ears and said, "I didn't hear that."

Anthony's words rang in my brain again. He told me to leave that side in prison, but how was I supposed to separate that person? I thought about Maria and what she said. I understood where she was coming from, but for her to feel that I wasn't justified for being this way was crazy. I don't think anyone could go through what I went through and still have any kind of sanity left. I thought I was doing well because I hadn't gone completely crazy.

Paul finished raiding the fridge and left. He gave me another five thousand dollars. I asked him what was it for, and he told me that it was spending money. I informed him that I still had all but seventy dollars of the last five he gave me. He didn't seem to care. He said that he was told to give me the money, so he gave me the money. I asked him where it came from, but he wouldn't say. He just put the envelope on the table, grabbed his food and left.

22

For the next four months, I just relaxed in the hotel. I would go out from time to time to get something to eat or just go to a movie. My stitches had healed up and I no longer had problems with the wounds bleeding or splitting open. Dr. Bowman had done an excellent job of sewing me up.

Paul continually stopped by. He would bring me money about twice a month, the usual five thousand. I saved most of it. Out of the forty-five thousand that he gave me, I had forty-four and some change left. I didn't have to pay rent, and I didn't have to really buy anything except food. Sometimes I didn't even have to buy food because Paul would show up with four or five bags of it.

I hadn't talked with Maria since that last conversation in her office. I had come to realize that she was right; I was different. I mean, I still acted civilized, but I had a very short temper. I didn't go off and kill people like in prison, but there were times that I wanted to. That was how I was so different. Before jail, I couldn't even see myself hurting another person. After jail, I could do it and not even think twice about it.

Paul had filed the lawsuit with the courts during my first week out of prison. We had received a court date of December 4, 2011, which came before I knew it. I knew that I was going to court for something in my favor, but I still wasn't anxious to go.

Paul did just as I thought he would. During the jury selection, he tried to eliminate every man from the jury. He was pretty successful. The jury was composed of ten women and two men, with two female alternates.

Paul controlled the trial for the first couple of days. He showed the jury the pictures that were taken in the hotel. He ripped apart the investigation. I think he wanted to do that during the first trial, but he had been playing defense. Now that he was on offense, he was tearing apart everything they said, did and even thought.

It was about a week into the trial and Paul was ready to wrap up his case against the State. It was the night before his last day of calling witnesses. Paul was working at his office at his desk as I laid on his couch. Paul was pretty confident that we were going to win, but he didn't want to leave anything to chance. He told me to go home. He said that it was going to be a long night for him and after staying with him for some of his long nights, I decided to go get something to eat and go back to the hotel.

Paul let me have one of his cars and I drove that back to the hotel. He had taken me to get my driver's license a few months back. When I went to look for a little car to drive, just to get me around town, he gave me his. I told him I would pay him for it, but he wouldn't take the money. He wouldn't even let me put gas in the car.

I decided to stop past this burger restaurant on my way back to the hotel. I walked inside and got in line. I heard people laughing and children playing all throughout the restaurant. I was looking up at the menu, trying to decide between a double cheeseburger with regular fries or a bacon cheeseburger with curly fries, when I felt someone watching me.

I looked down from the menu to see a little girl, no older than thirteen, staring at me with a stunned expression on her face. I tried not to look, so I glanced back up at the menu, only to feel her eyes lock on me more. She was a pretty little girl, but she was very young. I knew that I had been in prison for a long time, but nowhere near *that* long.

When I could no longer ignore her, I looked at her and asked, "Are you okay?"

She didn't respond, but just stood there looking at me.

I walked over to her and asked, "Are you okay? Are you looking for someone? Are you lost?"

She looked at me, perplexed, like I was a scrambled up puzzle or something.

"Sweetie, is your mother here?" I asked.

She shook her head yes.

"Okay, where is she?"

She pointed around the corner.

"Is she sitting at a table around there?" I asked her, wanting to make sure her mother was in the restaurant.

She shook her head yes.

"Okay. Well I think it would be best if you went back over to her," I said.

"No," she said. She shook her head slightly, but didn't take her eyes off of me.

I didn't know what to do. This little girl was just staring at me in the middle of the restaurant.

"Okay. Well, I am going to order my food. You have a good day." I walked off and got back in line. She stood there looking at me. When the people in front of me were finished, I walked up to the cashier to place my order.

"Yeah, I would like to have a number one with curly fries and a Coke." I had decided on the bacon cheeseburger because the picture looked awesome.

"Okay, sir. That will be a number one with curly fries and a large Coke?" the cashier asked.

"Yes," I responded.

"Okay, that will be......."

Before he could finish, the little girl tapped me on the arm. Startled, I turned to look at her and said, "Yes, little lady."

"Who are you?" she asked, standing right next to me.

I didn't know how to answer that question. I really didn't know who or what she was looking for.

The cashier started over, "That will be four dollars and fifty-seven cents."

I reached into my back pocket and pulled out my wallet. I gave the cashier a twenty and stepped to the side to wait for my change and the food.

The little girl stepped aside with me and asked me once again, "Who are you?"

"Are you looking for someone?" I asked.

She shook her head no.

"Okay, I really think it would be a good time for you to go back to your mother," I said, feeling very uncomfortable about how this situation looked.

The cashier gave me my change and my food. I thanked him and walked over to the condiments counter to grab some ketchup, napkins and a straw. I wanted to leave the restaurant, but the little girl was just standing there staring at me. I stopped when I got to the door, turned around and walked back over to her.

"Come on, let's go back to your mother."

I put my food and drink in my left hand and grabbed her hand. We walked back around the corner.

"Where is your mother, sweetie?"

The little girl pointed to a woman in the corner. She was sitting down with a man who appeared to be her husband and a very young child who looked about two to three years in age.

We started to walk over towards the woman until I got a good look at her. I stopped, but the little girl kept walking. When she noticed I had stopped, she turned around and pulled my hand towards her, signaling for me to come on.

I pulled her hand for her to follow me. We walked back around the corner and sat down at a table. I stared at her, harder than she was staring at me.

"Who are you?" I asked.

"Who are you?" she asked back.

"What is your name?" I asked her.

"What is your name?" she asked back.

Feeling like this was getting us nowhere, I asked, "Why were you staring at me?"

"Because I know you, but I don't know who you are."

"How do you know me?" I asked.

"Because I have dreamt about you so many times, I could never forget your face. You used to come to see me in my dreams all the time when I was a little girl, but then you stopped. Months ago, you came to see me again. My therapist said that you were a made-up person, but I knew that you were real."

I sat there, confounded. I didn't know what to do or say.

"And that woman, that is your mother?"

"Yes."

"And that man is your father?"

"No, my father is in prison. My mother said he killed a woman."

I shook my head no, I couldn't believe this. My emotions were racing as I continued to look at her.

"Do me a favor, please?" She shook her head yes. "Move your hair on the right side of your head, and turn your neck towards me.

She moved her hair and as she turned her neck, my heart dropped. I saw a birthmark, THE birthmark. Crystal had a birthmark on that side of her neck.

"What is your name?" I demanded.

"Kris. What is your name?" she asked.

"Kris? Is that what your mother calls you?"

"Yes, why?"

"What is your real name?"

"Crystal," she said.

I dropped my head to the table. I had my hands covering my face so that I could try to regain my composure without scaring her off.

"Your birthday is December 21st. You were born in 2000 at Children's Hospital. You have a birthmark on the right side of your neck and the left side of your stomach. Your mother's name is Emily and I know how you know me."

"How?" she asked with tears running down her face. I didn't know if she was crying because she was scared or happy.

"Because Crystal Aleaha Sutton, I am Jim...your father."

We just sat there for awhile. My brain was racing! How on earth could she be alive? What body did they find? She just sat there with tears rolling down her face. At least ten minutes passed before we both heard a familiar voice.

"Kris, where are you?" Emily shouted as she walked around the corner.

The guy she was with yelled from around the corner. "She probably ran away," he said as he laughed.

Emily laughed herself and said, "I wish she would. It would be one less headache I would have to worry about."

Just then she saw her sitting at the table, but she didn't recognize me. She walked over to us.

"Crystal, get your butt up! What are you doing sitting here with this grown man?"

I looked at Crystal and said, "Don't you move."

Emily looked at me and said, "Excuse me, this is my daughter."

I jumped out of my seat and grabbed her by the throat. "NO, she is MY daughter!" I screamed.

Emily instantly went into shock. She just stood there, trying to gasp for air. Every eye in the restaurant was on us. Her friend came around the corner with the child in his arms.

"Hey, what is going on here? Get your hands off my wife," he said as he put the child down and ran over to us.

"This is my wife and if you touch me I will kill her," I said, not even looking at him. I stared directly into Emily's eyes, feeding off of her fear.

"Daddy," Crystal said, "let her go. Come on daddy, let her go."

I told Crystal to get her stuff so we could go. I pushed Emily backwards and she fell over a chair and onto the floor. I grabbed Crystal's hand and we walked out of the restaurant. Emily came running outside screaming, "I am going to call the police!"

I laughed at her and questioned, "And tell them what, that I kidnapped my daughter who has been dead for about six years?"

Her friend ran outside and stood between the car and us. This guy must have missed the memo about me, but he was about to find out firsthand, real fast.

Emily picked up the child and yelled to the man, "Maurice, please don't let him take my baby."

He stood there, looking like he was ready to fight. "Dude, I do not know who you are, but you are not taking Kris!"

I laughed at him and tried to walk around him. He jumped in my way and kept saying, "You are not taking her. You are not taking her."

When I attempted to walk around him again, he pushed me back and tried to take my hand away from Crystal's. I couldn't even put the rage I felt into words. If Chuck, the guy from prison, had poured a gallon of milk into a shot glass, this guy had just poured two gallons into a thimble.

I was holding Crystal's hand with my left one, so I swung at him with my right and struck him in the face. He fell backwards into the car, which was the only reason he didn't hit the ground. He came back at me and punched me on the left side of my face, connecting with my jaw. I brushed it off like it was nothing. I was so angry, I was like a man high on cocaine who could get shot forty times but never feel it. Being that I felt invincible even to a bullet, his punch did absolutely nothing but piss me off more.

I let go of Crystal's hand and struck him again. He fell into the car again, but this time I didn't wait for him to come back. I pounced on him like a lion on a gazelle. I hit him over and over again until he fell to the ground unconscious. As soon as he hit the ground, Emily ran over to try to grab Crystal. I turned around as soon as I heard Crystal scream, "Get off me!"

Emily was screaming and crying, "Leave us alone! Just leave us alone!"

I walked over to her and said coldly, "If you do not let my daughter go, I will kill him and the child."

Emily stood there, holding onto the child and to Crystal. I walked over to her and grabbed the little boy out of her arm and picked him up in the air by his throat. I stood there, choking the little boy to death as Emily contemplated releasing Crystal to me.

As the little boy's face turned blue, she pushed Crystal towards me and ran over to grab him. I dropped him from the air and grabbed Crystal's hand. He fell, hit the ground and started screaming as Emily ran over to him. Emily was infuriated, but when he screamed I felt relieved, because at least I knew he was breathing. I didn't want him to die, but I wouldn't have given it a second thought if he had to.

Emily ran over and picked him up. She started cursing at me as Crystal and I walked over to my car to leave. I picked up Maurice and threw him into the grassy area in front of the car. I got in a few kicks before I walked back to the car, unlocked it and drove off with Crystal. Emily was walking over towards him as I pulled off.

We drove down the street and headed towards the hotel. As we were driving down the road, we saw police flying on the opposite side of the street.

Crystal leaned over to me and said, "They are coming for you."

I grabbed her hand and kissed it. I said, "Don't worry baby, it will be okay."

Crystal looked at me with tears coming to her eyes and said, "You can't leave me again."

I looked at her and smiled. I replied, "I won't."

"You promise?" she asked.

"I promise."

I drove to the hotel and pulled into the parking lot. We sat in the car for a second just looking at each other, then we drove off.

"Where are we going?" she asked.

"We are going to see a friend," I responded.

We pulled up to the Police Station. I told Crystal to go inside and give a message to a Detective Diaz.

Crystal said okay, opened the door and walked inside. She walked to the front desk and asked to speak to Detective Diaz. The officer in the front ran to the back office where she was. He spoke to Maria for a second, then signaled with his hand for Crystal to come to the back. She walked past the rows of desks and into Maria's office. Maria was sitting behind her desk with a folder opened and a cup of coffee in her hand.

"Are you Detective Diaz?" Crystal asked.

"Yes, I am. How may I help you?" Maria asked as she sipped her coffee and looked at the folder.

"I have a message for you from my dad."

"Oh. Well, you sure are here pretty late," Maria said, looking at her watch and noticing that is was almost ten o'clock. "Is your dad here?" Maria asked.

"Yes, he is outside," Crystal said.

"Well, would he like to come in and talk with me?"

"No. He just told me to give you a message."

Maria motioned for her to sit down in one of the chairs in her office. Crystal walked over to the chair and sat down.

"Okay, honey. So what's the message?"

"Justified."

"Justified?" Maria questioned puzzled. "What does that mean?"

"I do not know Ms. Diaz, he just told me to tell you that."

Maria sat in the chair for a moment and kept repeating the word to herself. She just couldn't figure it out.

"Justified?" Maria asked again.

"Yes, ma'am. All he said was justified."

Maria was still confused. We hadn't talked in months and by now she had forgotten the conversation that we had in her office.

Crystal stood up and announced, "Okay, I have to go now."

Maria stood up and said, "Wait, I will walk you out."

Maria put her arm around Crystal as they walked through the Police Station. Maria kept trying to figure out what that word meant and who would send this girl to tell her that. They walked through the front door and down the steps. Crystal ran to the passenger side of the car as Maria stood at the bottom of the steps. I opened my door and got out. Maria looked at me, surprised. She walked over to me.

"What are you doing here?"

"Did you get my message?"

"Yeah, 'justified', what does that have....." she stopped. The memory of our last conversation entered her brain. She looked at me with anger growing in her eyes.

"Are you still trying to prove that what you did was okay? It will never be okay with me."

"I never wanted it to be okay with you, I just want you to understand why I did what I did. I don't care if you agree with it, just understand it."

Maria looked off. No matter how she played out the situation in her brain, she knew that I wasn't wrong for killing them. She looked over at Crystal and asked, "And who is she?"

I looked at Crystal with pride in my eyes and proclaimed, "That is my daughter."

Maria looked back at me and said, "I thought you only had one daughter."

"I do."

Maria looked at me, looked back at Crystal, then looked back at me and asked, "Is that her?"

My eyes watered up as I replied, "Yeah, that's her."

Maria started crying instantly as she put her hand over her mouth.

"Crystal, come here, baby," I said. She walked around the car and to my side. She wrapped her arms around me and rested her head on my ribs. I put my arm around her and hugged her tight.

"Crystal, this is Detective Maria Diaz. Maria, this is Crystal Sutton, my daughter."

Maria could no longer control her emotions and the tears poured down her face. She tried to speak as clearly as possible, "Could I give her a hug?" she asked.

I looked at Crystal. "She is okay," I told her.

Crystal let go of me and walked over to Maria. Maria hugged her tighter than I did. The sight of the two of them together started to get to me. It was crazy, but I felt the human side of me trying to return.

I looked at Maria. "She needs oxygen," I said, smiling.

Maria backed up and said, "Oh, I am sorry." She wiped her face with her hand, trying to dry the tears. "I am so sorry."

"It's okay," I said.

Just then a police car pulled up and the window went down. A black cop was sitting on the passenger side. He called out, "Detective!"

Maria wiped her face a couple more times then turned to him and said, "Yes."

"Did you hear about what happened in Pineville?"

"No, what happened?"

"This guy went crazy and attacked this family at the fast food place off of Stone Avenue. He beat the guy up pretty bad; the mother and child only had minor bruises."

Maria looked at me as she asked the officer, "Did they get a description of the guy?"

"They are over there now interviewing the staff at the restaurant. I am sure they are going to get the tape from the surveillance camera. They will have him pretty soon."

Maria looked back at him and stated, "Man, that's crazy. I am glad that didn't happen in our jurisdiction. I'd hate to run into that guy tonight." Maria looked back at me. "There is no telling what I would do to someone like him."

"Yeah, I know what you mean. I would love to meet that low life. I will tell you one thing, I wouldn't arrest him, that's for sure. I would beat the ......"

I jumped in, "I'm sorry, I haven't introduced myself. My name is Jim, and yours?"

"Jay, Jay Seltzer," he said, extending his hand out the window to shake mine.

"Nice to meet you, Jay," I said, shaking his hand.

"Nice to meet you too, Jim."

"Alright," Maria said. "I will see you inside."

"Okay Detective, see you later," he said as the car pulled off.

Maria looked at me and demanded, "What happened?"

"It's a long story and I think we have overstayed our welcome. I will tell you later."

Maria bent down to Crystal and gave her one last hug. Then she gave her a kiss on the cheek. "You take care of yourself, okay?" she said, with another tear running down her face. Crystal shook her head yes.

She stood up and smacked me across the face. "You make me SO angry!"

I laughed it off, but Crystal walked in between me and her. Maria looked down at her and tried to soften her facial expression.

"Excuse me, honey, your daddy and I have to talk."

Crystal didn't move. She just stood there looking at her.

Maria looked at her, then looked at me, "I will talk to you when your bodyguard is not around," she said.

"I am not protecting him," Crystal said, "I am protecting you."

I bent down and gave Crystal a kiss on the cheek. "I am okay baby, you can get in the car."

Crystal looked at me with fear in her eyes and asked, "Are you sure?"

"Yes, I am sure."

She gave me a kiss on my cheek, then whispered into my ear, "I am not a baby."

I laughed as she walked around the car and opened the door. Once she was in the car with the door closed, Maria walked right up to me, and put her face two inches away from mine.

"She was protecting me? What in the world happened and why did she look like you were about to kill me?"

"Because she just saw what happened to the last person that touched me."

Maria looked into the car and saw Crystal staring at us. "Where are you going?" she questioned.

"Back to the hotel that I have been staying at. We are going to stay there for the night. I will figure out the rest in the morning."

"I will follow you. Let me go grab my stuff. I'll be right back." Maria leaned in and slowly put her lips on mine, pressing them gently together. She leaned back and smiled, "I am so happy for you."

She ran into the police station and moments later she ran back out with her coat. She went to her car as I got back into mine. As I started the car up, I felt Crystal's eyes locked on me. I knew what she was thinking. "Go ahead," I said.

"YUCK!" she said, then burst into laughter.

I had to laugh myself. It felt good that she was back; and even better, it seemed like nothing had changed.

23

We arrived back at the hotel and went straight up to the room. When Maria and Crystal walked into the room, their mouths fell wide open. Maria walked around the room about four or five times. Crystal walked in and looked at everything. She looked at the sitting area, the bedroom and the bathroom in amazement. She would have walked around just as much as Maria if she hadn't found my endless supply of chocolate in one of the refrigerators. She couldn't even speak, she just grabbed a handful and looked at me for approval.

"Go ahead," I said with a smile on my face.

Maria walked into the sitting area and asked, "How in the world can you afford this?"

"Don't ask, it's a long story."

Maria looked at me and said, "Well, what do you think I am here for?"

We all gathered in the sitting area and sat down. Maria sat in the chair straight in front of me. Crystal sat on the couch and I sat in the chair that was to the right of Crystal.

Crystal had laid all of her chocolate out on the couch. She had just finished off her second candy bar when she noticed Maria and I staring at her.

She picked up a candy bar. "Would you like one?" she asked Maria, handing it to her.

"Yes, thank you." Maria took the candy bar, unwrapped it and started eating it.

Maria had taken two bites before she looked up at me and asked, "How is this possible?"

"I don't know, but we are about to find out."

Crystal put the chocolate down and looked at the both of us.

"Where have you been?" I asked her.

"California," she said. "We live out there with Maurice."

"Do you remember what happened the day you disappeared?" Maria asked.

She shook her head no. "Not really," she said. "All I know is that I was sad all the time."

"How do you know that?" I asked.

"Mommy took me to a therapist because of it. She told him that I was having problems adjusting to the move. He gave me these pills that I had to take every day to get rid of my sadness."

I put my head down because I couldn't believe what I just heard. Emily took Crystal from me and she had the nerve to act like Crystal was the problem. I tried to calm myself down because I had a lot more questions to ask.

Maria saw that I was getting upset, so she tried to change the subject.

"Well, why did you come all the way back here?"

"Maurice's mother got sick. We came back to see her."

"His mother lives in Pineville?" I questioned.

"No, she lives in Scottsdale, by where we used to live. Well, that is what mommy said."

"What were you doing in Pineville?" Maria asked.

"We were on our way back to the airport." Crystal said, biting a piece of candy.

My anger level was rising fast. Maria could see that and decided to change the subject again.

"How did you find each other?" Maria asked.

Crystal was about to talk, but I cut her off. "Are you asking as a cop or a friend?"

Maria picked up the pillow that was in the chair and threw it at me. She replied, "A friend, you jerk!"

The pillow landed innocently on the floor as Crystal laughed. I nodded my head for Crystal to go ahead and tell her.

"I saw him walk in," she started. "And after I saw him, I asked mommy could I get some ketchup. She said I could, so I walked around the corner and just stood there looking at him. He didn't know who I was, and I didn't know who he was, I just knew his face."

"His face?" Maria asked. "How did you know his face? You haven't seen him in almost six years."

Crystal looked at me and smiled. She said, "I dreamt about him. He used to come and see me all of the time when I slept. I could never forget his face."

Maria sat back in the chair. I knew she believed Crystal, but I also knew that what Crystal was saying was extremely unbelievable.

Crystal jumped up and grabbed a bag that she was carrying with her. "Would you like to see my journal?"

"Sure," Maria said.

Crystal handed the journal to Maria. Maria opened up the book and started to flip through the pages. She started from the beginning, reading page after page. She came to a page in the book that caught her eye. She read it for minute then asked Crystal, "What does this mean?" She handed the book to Crystal and pointed to the part she was talking about. Crystal looked at the page and then a tear rolled down her cheek.

"My therapist said to write down when I have bad dreams. This is one of those really bad dreams that I had."

Concerned, I looked at her and asked, "What happened?"

Crystal really started to cry now as she responded, "You went away." She dropped the book, walked over to me and sat on my lap. I put my arms around her as she cried. "You can't leave me again," she said.

"I won't, baby, I promise."

She cried for a couple more minutes and then got up. I made sure she was okay and told her that if she didn't feel like talking, we could stop. It was already a quarter to twelve anyway, but she wanted to keep going.

She sat down and picked up the book. Maria wiped her face with a tissue because she was crying as well and handed the box to

Crystal. Crystal took a couple of tissues and put the box on the coffee table.

She opened the book back up to the page Maria was asking her about and started to explain what happened on that day.

"I had a dream that I was laying on a bed in this big room. Everything was white - the walls, the sheets, everything. You came through the door and I was happy. You walked over to me, gave me a kiss, said I love you and turned to walk away. I asked you where you were going. You told me that you were going away. Then blood started coming through your shirt and your eyes closed. I screamed for you to open your eyes. I yelled at you that you couldn't leave me, but you were. The white walls turned black and darkness started to swallow you. I prayed for God to save you," she said, with tears running down her face.

"I must have been yelling in real life, because mommy woke me up. She said that I was having a nightmare."

Tears were flowing down Maria's face. She sat up and grabbed the box of tissue off the coffee table.

"Mommy took me to the therapist and he gave me this book. I have been writing down my dreams ever since. The first couple of pages I just wrote for fun, but the rest of the pages are all of the dreams I had."

Maria asked to see the book back and Crystal handed it to her. Maria looked at the page. "August 12, 2006," she said, turning the page.

"What was that date?" I asked, remembering what Dr. Bowman said when I first got out of prison.

"August 12, 2006," Maria said.

I looked at Crystal as tears came to my eyes, "I am sorry. I am so sorry."

Maria and Crystal looked confused. They had no idea what had just happened.

"Maria, look through the book to see if she had a bad dream on November 6, 2007."

Maria flipped through the book really fast. I got up and walked into the bedroom to find my medical records from the hospital. Maria kept searching as I walked back into the sitting room with the papers in my hand.

"You don't have to look," Crystal said. "I think I had the exact same dream on that day."

As Crystal was finishing her statement, Maria found the page.

"Yes you did, but how did you remember that?" Maria asked.

"Because I read that journal a lot," Crystal replied.

Maria looked at me and asked, "Well, how did you know about that day?"

I handed Maria the papers from the prison. She glanced over the papers for a second and looked back at me. "What am I looking for?" she asked.

I pointed to the place where it stated I had passed away - twice. Maria's jaw dropped as she read it.

"YOU DIED TWICE!" Maria shouted.

"Yes, on the exact same dates of your dreams," I said to Crystal.

Crystal's eyes began to release tear after tear. "You died?" she asked, running over to hug me.

"Yes sweetie, but I am here now."

I don't think she heard that part. All she heard was that I had been dead and the fear from her dream was confirmed as reality. She squeezed me tight and wasn't about to let go. I tried to walk, but she wasn't having it. So we stood there for about ten minutes, with her hugging and squeezing me. She wasn't trying to let go, and I didn't blame her one bit.

The pressure from her squeezing me eventually took its toll on her arms. She began to get weak, but that didn't stop her from trying. I slowly began to walk to the couch. She followed while still holding onto me. I removed her arms, gave her a kiss, and sat her down. I walked back to my chair as she watched me.

Maria didn't know what to say. It seemed that every time she changed the subject, someone started crying. She looked at me with a blank expression on her face; she didn't know what to do. She flipped through the book, looking to find something that could spark a good memory. She came to a page and smiled.

"Crystal," Maria said, "this appears to be a good dream." Maria pointed to a page in the book with flowers and smiley faces drawn all around it. I looked at the page from across the table and smiled myself. It appeared to be a happy page and so did the page next to it.

Crystal, on the other hand, put her head down and appeared to be fighting back tears. Maria looked at me, dumbfounded. We were both at a loss for words, but Maria was frustrated by the fact that everything she brought up just made Crystal feel worse.

Maria read the first couple of sentences on the page.

"Crystal," she said. "This passage was during the summer when you were seven. It seems that your dreams were really good."

Crystal looked up and admitted, "Yeah, they were."

"Well, what happened?" I asked.

"You came to see me every night. You would come lay with me, stroke my hair and sing to me. I would wake up every morning happy, and I was excited to go to sleep at night. I saw you everyday for a week and everything was fine. Then one day, I had a dream that you were sitting in a corner and crying. I walked over to you to comfort you, but no matter what I did, you wouldn't stop crying. I hugged you and I sang to you, but you just kept crying and apologizing to me."

A tear rolled down her face. Maria started to cry also.

"The next day I had a dream about you in a dark room, locked in a cage. It was you, but it wasn't you. He had your face, but the eyes were like that of a dog or a wolf. I felt really scared and I knew something was wrong, but I didn't know what. Then all of a sudden, the cage door opened and you walked out. But it wasn't you, it was someone else."

Crystal grabbed some tissue and wiped her face.

"I didn't dream about you or see you for about three and a half years after that. Then six months ago, you came to see me again to tell me you were free. That was the last time I dreamt about you."

Maria realized the story Crystal told was related to when she gave me the picture and the prisoners took it. She got up and walked over to me. She leaned in, gave me a kiss on my cheek and whispered into my ear, "Justified." She understood what happened. She understood how I felt and what that picture meant not only to me, but to Crystal as well.

I looked at the clock and realized that it was going on one o'clock and Crystal was tired, probably from all of the crying. I gave her a hug and told her to get into my bed to go to sleep. She made me promise that I was going to be there in the morning, and I did promise. Crystal asked me to come and lay with her until she fell asleep. Maria waited in the sitting room as I went with Crystal to put her to bed. I laid beside her and sang to her until she fell asleep, just like old times.

Crystal was asleep in a couple of minutes because she was so tired. I laid beside her for awhile staring at her. Eventually, I went back into the front room and Maria was sprawled out on the couch. I walked in and sat down in the chair she was sitting in.

"I know your man is looking for you."

Maria sat up. "You are sad," she said, smiling.

"What? I was just making a statement."

She got up and walked over to me. She sat down on my lap sideways and gave me a slow, sweet kiss on my lips. Once she finished, she leaned back and looked at me. "Does that answer your question?" she asked.

I smiled and asked, "So how long have you been cheating on him?"

Maria laughed and went to get up. I pulled her arm and she fell back into my lap, laughing.

I stared into her eyes for a moment and questioned, "Why didn't you come and see me?"

Maria stared back at me and replied, "Because I was mad at you. You weren't the man that I fell in love with, but I understand now and I want to apologize."

I looked at her, trying to comprehend what she just said to me.

"Don't give me that look," she said, smiling. "I want to apologize because I really didn't understand what happened to you. If I had known it caused you that much pain, then I wouldn't have acted like that. You really didn't deserve that. So, I am sorry from the bottom of my heart. Though I may not agree with what you did, I understand why you did it."

"Well, thank you Ms. Diaz, and your apology is accepted."

Maria turned around and looked into the bedroom. "You have some kind of bond with that little girl," she said, turning her head back towards me. "That is just amazing. Even when you two were miles apart, you were still together."

I looked into the room myself and said, "I know, that is my heart in there. I just can't believe she is alive," I said, smiling.

Maria looked at me confused and asked, "What body did they find?"

I looked back at her confused also and responded, "I have no idea. Whoever it was, it wasn't her." It hit me that some other child must have been killed and sorrow entered my heart for the first time in years. Someone's parents have gone through what I have gone through, but they don't get their baby back. Their little girl is gone forever. As my human side returned, I couldn't help but feel sorry for them.

Maria straddled me and asked, "What do you want to do?"

I looked at her smiling and returned the question, "What do you want to do?'

She leaned in, put her hands on the back of the chair and gave me a kiss. "It's okay, you can touch me." I put my hands on her waist nervously. She smiled and leaned in to kiss me again. As her lips connected with mine, she opened up her mouth and gently moved her tongue up and down my tongue. My excitement level raised quickly. She moved back as she felt me rise and laughed a little.

"Well, I see what someone wants to do," she said, smiling.

"I'm sorry. It has been about seven years since I did something like this."

"Seven? You were only in prison for five and a half."

I laughed and admitted, "Emily and I stopped being together for a long time before I went to prison."

Maria smiled. "Well, it looks like somebody remembers how to do it," she said, referring to my excited state.

I grabbed the back of her head and slowly moved it close to mine. I kissed her on her cheek, then her other cheek, then her lips. I opened my mouth first this time and she opened hers. We kissed until "YUCK!" came from the bedroom.

Crystal laughed as she rolled over in the bed and grabbed a pillow to cover her face. Maria and I laughed as well.

"Go to sleep, woman!" I screamed into the bedroom.

"I am trying to, if you two could keep it down out there. Especially you, daddy," she said, laughing hard.

Maria looked at me and died laughing. I was embarrassed, but I had to laugh because it was very funny.

"Just go to sleep," I said through my laughter.

"Yes, Daddy."

Maria whispered to me, "I thought she was asleep."

"I thought she was too. Maybe she woke up."

Crystal yelled from the room, "I did wake up!"

Maria and I both shook our heads, smiling.

"I wanted to make sure you were still here," Crystal said.

I felt like the Grinch that Stole Christmas, everything Crystal said and did made my heart grow.

"I am not going anywhere, baby. You are safe. Now go to bed."

"I love you, Daddy."

"I love you too, baby."

The room got quiet for a couple of seconds. Maria and I looked at each other. She leaned in to kiss me again until, "I am not a baby," echoed from the room.

I laughed and yelled, "Go to bed!"

Maria laughed and then whispered into my ear, "Do you have a place where we can have a little more privacy?"

I looked around the room and replied, "No, I'm sorry, but this is it."

She looked around the room, "Let's go in here." She grabbed me and pulled me into the bathroom. She locked the door, turned on the shower for background noise and turned off the light. I felt around in the dark for her. Once I found her, I noticed that my hand only touched skin - all of her clothes were gone. I proceeded to kiss her as she undressed me. I picked her up and put her on the countertop. I knew that it was cold, but she didn't seem to care, so neither did I. I entered her and she let out a moan. I stroked slowly, going in and out of her. She had her arms around my neck and she moaned quietly, trying not to be too loud. I made love to her for all of ninety seconds. I apologized to her for it being such a short time. I even used the excuse that it had been seven years, but she told me not to worry about it and that it was perfect.

We stayed in the bathroom, kissing and holding each other. After a couple of minutes, my excitement level raised again. We made love again. This time around, it lasted much longer and she was unable to be as quiet as she was the first time. The first time around, I had exploded in a short time; the next time, she exploded in a short time, repeatedly. She apologized and even used the excuse that it had been years since she was with someone. I told her not to worry about it, that it was perfect. "Besides, when you mess with the master, things like that are going to happen," I joked. She laughed and asked for the master again, and she got it. We made love four times that night. When we finally finished, it was 6:30 in the morning.

We washed off in a shower that had nothing but cold water left. We got dressed and snuck out of the bathroom, hardly able to walk. I sat down for about two minutes, and then I heard the phone ring.

"Hello," I said, tired and extremely sore. In the middle of the third time, she had started to lock up a little bit. I told her that we could stop, but she didn't want to. We finished that time and went one more. That would explain why she was laying on the couch with her legs padlocked together.

"Are you ready?" It was Paul.

"Ready for what?" I asked.

"What? What do you think?" he said.

"Oh no, I forgot!" I said as I jumped up. In all of the excitement of the night, going to court had totally slipped my mind.

"You forgot? How in the world could you forget about court?"

"I will explain to you later."

"Alright, don't be late. You have to be there by nine o'clock."

"Okay, see you there."

I got off the phone with Paul and fell into the chair. Maria was already asleep and I felt bad for having to wake her up.

"Sweetheart, come on. We have to go."

Maria looked at me, eyes half opened and asked, "Go where?"

"To court," I said.

"For what?"

"Paul is suing the state for wrongful imprisonment."

Maria turned back over and mumbled, "So."

"It's for one hundred million dollars."

Her eyes opened up wide and she asked incredulously, "One hundred million? What?" She was stuck for a minute as she sat up. "Can he win?"

I looked at her with confidence and responded, "He said we should get around fifty; and yes, he will win because he doesn't lose."

Maria got up and got ready to go. I went and got Crystal up so she could get ready. We walked out of the door at eight o'clock to go to the courthouse. All the way to the elevator, I kept laughing at Maria.

When curiosity finally got the best of her, she turned around and asked, "What is so funny?"

"Finding it a little difficult to walk?" I asked.

She punched me in my arm and replied, "That's okay, revenge is sweet."

I smacked her on her butt and the impact made her lower body vibrate. She laughed as the pain rushed through her body.

"You jerk," she said as she leaned on the wall and tried to deal with the pain.

Crystal was still half asleep, so she really wasn't into the conversation. When we got to the elevator, she leaned on me and hugged me. I kissed Maria on her forehead as I hugged her with my right arm, and held Crystal with my left. For the first time in years, I was happy.

24

We arrived at the courthouse at ten minutes to nine. We stopped and grabbed a bite to eat. Crystal was awake now, after drinking a cola and eating some chocolate. I knew that it wasn't good for her to have for breakfast, but I haven't seen her in years. She could have anything she wanted.

Maria was up and running also. She had a double order of coffee to get her through the day. She drank most of it on the way to the courthouse. By the time we arrived, she was bouncing off the walls.

By this time, I wasn't even tired. I had slept for the last five months, so I really wasn't deprived of sleep.

I walked into the courtroom, told them to sit in the back and stay hidden, and walked up to sit with Paul. The judge came in, sat down and ordered Paul to call any other witness that he may have had.

After Paul went through the line of questions he had for his last witness and after the defense went through their questions, Paul stood up to say that the prosecution rested. Just as he was about to speak, I tapped him on his arm.

"Your honor, one second please," Paul said, then sat down to talk with me.

"What's wrong?" Paul asked.

"You have to call one more witness," I said.

"Why?" Paul asked.

"You just do! Please, just do it for me."

"Okay, what am I supposed to ask this witness?"

"Paul, are you the best?" I asked him.

Paul smiled and answered, "You know I am."

"Then you will know what to ask."

Paul looked at me with hesitation, but stood up and announced, "Your honor, the prosecution would like to call one more witness."

The judge nodded in approval.

Paul looked down at me and asked, "What is the witness' name?"

"Not yet," I said. "Just ask Detective Diaz to bring the witness up."

Paul made the announcement and Maria got up. Maria walked up front with a beautiful, brown-skinned little ten year old girl with beautiful long hair and pretty brown eyes. She got up on the stand and was sworn in.

Paul walked up to her and stood there for a moment, trying to find the right question to ask. He looked back at me and moved his lips to say the word "now".
I nodded my head to let him know it was time.

Paul turned to her and questioned, "Can you please state your name for the record?"

She leaned in and spoke into the microphone, "Crystal Aleaha Sutton."

The courtroom went into an uproar. The jury was stunned and the defense kept screaming, "Objection!"

Once the judge got the courtroom under control, Paul asked for her to state her name again. Again she said, "Crystal Aleaha Sutton."

Everyone in the courtroom had their mouths opened, including Paul. He stood there, trying to find the right words to say and the right question to ask.

Finally he asked, "Ms. Sutton, I thought you were murdered by your father."

Crystal smiled and replied, "My daddy would never do anything like that."

Reality finally caught up with the defense as he interjected, "Objection, your honor! How do we know that this is really Crystal

Sutton? We have documentation that Crystal was murdered. We have physical evidence."

Paul laughed and said, "Well, your honor, if it's the same evidence they used in the first trial, we have already determined in the appeal that they never had any."

The judge recessed the court until a determination could be reached as to whether or not this was really Crystal Sutton. The courts did a blood test. They also ordered for the body that was believed to be hers to be dug up. Paul went to have the dental records re-examined. If the dental record wasn't Crystal's, who signed off on the records to say that it was?

After the blood test was done, I was approached by two officers. They said they had a warrant for my arrest for the assault on Maurice.

As they were about to handcuff me, I turned to Maria and requested, "You have to do something for me." Maria pulled out her badge and told the officers to give her a minute.

She pulled me to the side. She looked scared and looked like she was about to cry. "What do you want me to do?"

I kissed her on her cheek and said, "Baby, don't worry about this. Just let Paul know and I will be out before the day is over."

She said okay as she tried to shake off her fears.

"Baby," I said, trying to look into her eyes.

"I'm okay," she said, shaking her head as if trying to shake off her thoughts. "What do you need me to do?"

"Do not let Crystal out of your sight. She is not to leave your side, do you understand me?" I asked, hoping she picked up on my seriousness.

"She will not leave my side," she said.

"Promise me."

"I promise, sweetie," she said. She leaned into me and gave me a kiss on the lips. I kissed her back as the officers walked over to put the handcuffs on me.

"Hurry back, honey, we have a date tonight."

"We do?" I asked.

"Yeah, last night was just practice; I am ready for the real thing now," she said, laughing.

"You can barely walk now," I said, smiling.

"Whatever."

They walked me out of the door, booked me and sent me to a holding cell. I was arrested at twelve-fifteen and Paul had me out before one o'clock.

My bail was set at ten thousand dollars. I had to pay the ten percent in order to get out. When the judge read the amount, Paul instantly opened up his wallet and handed Maria the money. She walked out, holding Crystal's hand, to go and pay for my bail.

Once I made bail, we all got something to eat while we waited for the test results. We went to a little restaurant down the street from the courthouse. Paul sat next to me in the booth while Crystal sat on the inside next to Maria.

"Daddy, I saw Mommy at the courthouse."

"You did? When?" I asked.

"I saw her when they took you to jail," she said.

"Well, what did she say?" I inquired.

Maria jumped into the conversation, "She told Crystal to go with her."

I looked at Maria, "And, what happened?"

"I told her that Crystal was in police custody and that she would have to remain with me."

Paul laughed and asked, "And that worked?"

Maria looked at Paul and answered sharply, "Some people don't manipulate the law like others."

I looked at Maria and asked, "Is there something that I should know about?"

"No, just that your lawyer is the lowest of the low. He is lower than dirt."

Paul leaned over to me and whispered, "She is a little upset about a couple of my clients getting off. She thinks that they were guilty; I thought that they were insane. The jury believed insane and put them in a mental institution for ten years."

"They killed a cop," Maria interjected.

"They killed a cop who was dirtier than they were," Paul countered.

"That has nothing to do with it," Maria said. "He was still a cop and didn't deserve to die like that."

"How did he die?" Crystal asked.

Both of them got silent. When Crystal spoke, they both realized that they were in front of a child. That was something that had slipped their minds during their discussion.

"Well, you might as well finish the story," I said.

Maria turned to Crystal and was about to speak, but I cut her off, "Tell the story as it happened and don't include your opinion."

Maria rolled her eyes at me. "Anyway, as I was about to say," she said, looking only at Crystal. "A cop was murdered and this gentleman over here represented the people who killed him. He told the courts something that wasn't true and….."

Paul jumped in, "Objection your honor! That is her opinion, not a fact."

"Sustained," I said. "Ms. Diaz, please try to stick with the facts of the case."

Maria kicked me gently under the table as Crystal laughed.

She continued, "They shot the officer over forty times and this gentleman didn't want them to go to prison; because if they would have gone to prison, it would have been for the rest of their lives. Instead, they went to an institution for the mentally ill and got out of there in six months."

"Well, what can I say? They were healed," Paul said.

Crystal laughed at Paul. Then she spoke to Maria, "Well, he can't be that bad."

"Thank you," Paul said, "Get this little lady anything that she wants."

"Why do you say that?" Maria asked.

"Because without him, my daddy would still be in jail and I would be on my way back to California," Crystal said. "And you wouldn't be here, either. So, he is pretty good to me," she said, smiling at Paul.

"Any more questions?" I asked Maria.

"No, the State would like to drop all charges," Maria said, smiling.

We ordered our food as peace returned to the table. Maria was actually talking to Paul without an attitude. The food arrived, we ate and then left to go back to the courthouse. Once we arrived, Paul went to the judge's chambers to speak with him. Paul came back thirty minutes later and stated that we would reconvene at nine o'clock the next morning.

Maria had to go to work, so Crystal and I went back to the hotel. I got Crystal something to eat for the night, but she didn't eat it. Once we got back to the hotel, we both passed out; Crystal slept in the bed and I was on the couch. Later that night, Maria came by the hotel and stayed the night with us.

The date she had planned failed to take place. She was so exhausted when she arrived that when I went to go fix her a drink, she fell asleep. She looked so peaceful I didn't dare wake her. I gave her a kiss on her cheek and put covers over her to keep her warm. She woke up for a second, looked at me and said, "I love you."

"I love you too, baby."

Just then, a shout came from the bedroom, "She is not a baby!" Crystal said and laughed.

I shook my head and laughed as Maria looked at me and smiled, I think she was too tired to laugh. "I *am* your baby," she protested.

"You better be," I said. I got on my knees and gave her a kiss. She smiled and then got comfortable so she could go back to sleep. I got up off my knees and went to go to sleep in the chair. Crystal came out of the room and asked me to sleep with her, so I did. She slept in the bed and I slept on the floor beside her holding her hand, just like before.

25

The next day we went back to the courthouse. The DNA results were in and they confirmed that Crystal was my daughter. The autopsy came back as well and confirmed that the body they found wasn't Crystal, but a seven year old Italian girl. Paul presented all of the new information to the jury. The defense was overwhelmed and just gave up.

The jury deliberated for about two hours and came back with a verdict in our favor. They awarded me forty eight million dollars for pain and suffering.

We walked out of the courthouse happy, all except Paul. He was upset that he didn't win fifty like he projected. He kept mumbling under his breath all the way to the car. I told him it was okay and thanked him again for everything he had done for me. He tried to shake off his frustration and be polite with us before he left. He eventually came around when I offered to buy him a sandwich from the convenience store. He said that he was going to sue the store, because those sandwiches were addictive. He said that they had to be putting something in them.

We drove to the store to get Paul's food and we also got Crystal some sweet stuff to snack on. Maria went to work and Crystal and I followed Paul to his office. When we got there, Crystal went into a little room to watch television as Paul and I talked.

"So what are you going to do, multi-millionaire?" Paul asked as he pulled out the chair to his desk and sat down.

"You mean, I get some money after I pay my legal fees?" I asked, as I sat down in a chair in front of his desk.

Paul laughed, "I am expensive, but not that expensive."

"What's up Paul, what am I looking at?"

Paul pulled a notepad out of his briefcase. "You have a couple of options. One, you can take your money, minus my legal fees and go off into the sunset."

"Okay," I nodded, "How much would I have left?"

Paul looked at his pad and responded, "About thirty-five million, give or take a million."

I thought about it for a second. I could walk away with at least thirty-three million, worst-case scenario.

"Option two?" I asked.

"You can hire me for the rest of your life and you can hire me for anyone else you want to."

"What if you die? Do I get a refund?"

Paul laughed and said, "No, you get another lawyer who is as good as me or better, guaranteed."

"So, how much is it to be in this club?"

"Club?" Paul asked. "I believe the term that is used is to be an 'Untouchable'? It is ten million per person."

I lowered my head. Ten million dollars is a lot of money. I didn't lower my head to think about the money, but to think about what I was going to do with eighteen million dollars.

I looked up at Paul and said, "Give me eighteen million and I want Crystal, Maria and myself protected for as long as we live."

Paul looked into his briefcase and pulled out his checkbook. "Done," he stated.

He wrote me a check for eighteen million dollars. I asked him if he wanted reimbursement for the hotel, food and everything else.

He looked at me, smiled and said, "You just gave me thirty million dollars; believe me, I have been reimbursed. Besides, that is what the government is for. I will write off all of that. Now get out of here and go take that little girl somewhere now."

I couldn't do anything but smile as I said, "I guess I can't say that I am broke anymore."

"Yeah, that excuse is long gone," Paul said.

I was about to go get Crystal until I realized I never found out about the five thousand dollars that kept coming.

"Paul, where did the money come from?"

"What money?" he asked.

"The five thousand every other week, who sent it?"

"You didn't read the letter?"

I shook my head no. I had forgotten all about the letter. That letter was still sitting on the table by the door at the hotel.

"Let's just say that we have a mutual friend who felt bad about a lot of stuff that you went through in prison."

"Why, was he the cause of the stuff that I went through in prison?"

Paul just stared at me and replied, "I can't say, but you know the answer to that."

"Well, what do I owe him?"

"Nothing, he said to just give you the money out of his account whenever he told me to. So whenever he sent word, I went into his account and withdrew the money."

I turned around and walked away to get Crystal. "Tell Anthony I said thanks."

"You got it," Paul replied.

I went into the room to get Crystal and we left. I thought about Anthony a lot on the way home. I was upset at first because I knew all of the stuff I went through in prison was his fault. Then again, I am where I am now because of him. It was really a double-edged sword; I couldn't have the good if I hadn't gone through the bad.

Crystal and I went back to the hotel and relaxed for the rest of the day. That night, Maria came over to the hotel. She was very upset; I could tell by the way she banged on the door. I ran to the door and opened it.

"What is wrong with you, banging on the door like you are the police?"

"I *am* the police," she said, as she stormed into the room.

She dropped her bag in the chair, smiled and said hello to Crystal, then grabbed my arm and pulled me into the bathroom.

She closed the door and turned on the shower. I looked at her, puzzled, because I really didn't know what to do. I was going to crack a joke, but this didn't appear to be the time to do it.

"What did you do?" Maria asked.

I really didn't know how to answer that. "What are you talking about?" I asked.

"Where did you go last night?" Maria asked.

"Maria, what are you talking about?"

Maria flipped the lid down, then sat down on the toilet and lowered her head. "Jay was killed last night," she said.

"Who is Jay?" I asked.

"The officer that pulled up the other night in the police cruiser. I found out today that he was killed last night."

"The dude that was talking all of that junk? What in the world happened?"

"I don't know, they are investigating it now. I just can't believe that he was killed. I was just talking with him yesterday and now he is dead."

I walked over to her and hugged her. She hugged me back, but she wasn't crying. I guess being a police officer had raised her tolerance level for death.

We hugged for a moment. I released her and walked over to the shower to cut it off. She pulled my hand back towards her, "What are you doing?" she asked.

"Cutting off the shower. I didn't want to use all of the hot water again."

She pulled me back towards her. "Let it run for a minute," she said, right before she kissed me.

We kissed for a couple of minutes and were almost entirely out of our clothes before we heard a knock at the door.

"I have to use the bathroom," Crystal said.

"One second sweetie," I said, moving my mouth away from Maria's just long enough to answer her. I turned back towards Maria and whispered, "Come on baby, we have to let the child use the bathroom."

"Okay," Maria said, pulling down her panties.

"What are you doing?" I asked.

"Nothing," she said. She turned around and bent over the sink. "You got a minute?" she asked.

We were together, going as fast as possible. Even though it was rushed, it still felt good to the both of us that we could be together. Once we finished, we hurried to wash off and put on our clothes. We ran out of the bathroom to witness Crystal doing the greatest '*I have to pee*' dance of all time.

Crystal ran into the bathroom as we went into the sitting room and sat on the couch together.

Maria leaned over and gave me a kiss on the lips.

"You are the master, but you are slipping," she said and laughed.

"Hey, I only had thirty seconds," I said in my own defense.

"Well, you could have used them all," Maria struck back.

I laughed and said, "Well, I'm sorry about that."

Maria leaned in and said, "No, don't apologize. It was perfect."

"No, you are perfect," I said and kissed her on the lips.

"Yuck," Crystal said. She had opened the bathroom door just as I kissed Maria.

Maria looked up over the couch and called, "Come here, sweetie." Crystal walked over to the couch and sat next to me and Maria. Maria wrapped her arm around Crystal and Crystal leaned into her. "Do you not like it when your father and I kiss?" Maria asked.

Crystal laughed shyly.

"It's not that," I said. "She does that whenever she sees anyone kiss on the lips."

"Why?" they both asked at the same time.

I grabbed Crystal and pulled her up on my lap. She wrapped her arms around me and rested her head on my shoulder.

"When Crystal was very little, she would see Emily and me kiss on the lips. So, one day, she decided to try to kiss me on the lips. When she did, I turned away, screamed 'Yuck!' and acted like I was dying from the kiss. Ever since then, she always says yuck when she sees me kiss on the lips."

Crystal hugged me tight, feeling a little embarrassed. Maria grabbed Crystal and tried to pull her over to her; but Crystal was a little too heavy, so she just scooted over to Maria.

"So, you don't mind me kissing your daddy?" Maria asked.

"No," Crystal said shyly. Even if she did, I don't think she would have said it.

"Are you sure? If it makes you feel uncomfortable, I won't do it."

"Do you like him?" Crystal asked.

Maria smiled at her and responded, "He's okay. I mean, if he was taller, then we could talk."

Crystal laughed and said, "He is very tall."

"I know, sweetie. I was just playing, I love your father."

"He's a very good daddy," Crystal said. "Are you going to marry him?"

Just then, Maria's cell phone rang. She excused herself, went into the bedroom and took the call. She was on the phone for about ten minutes before she walked back into the sitting area.

"That was the station. They are going to press charges on Detective Chambers for falsifying evidence."

"The dental records…." I said.

"Yeah, it's the dental records. Apparently Chambers got one of his friends to sign the paper stating that they were Crystal's records. He never even went to see her dentist."

I borrowed Maria's cell phone and called Paul.

"Have you heard?" I asked him.

"About Detective Chambers," he replied. "Yeah, I have already placed the call. They are on it."

I knew what he meant. He had already called Anthony and he was in the process of making sure that Detective Chambers went to Greens.

"Okay," I said. "Talk to you later."

As soon as I hung up with Paul, Maria walked up to me and asked, "So, are you going to marry me?"

My heart had stopped for a second because I thought she was going to ask about the conversation that I just had.

"As soon as I get a divorce," I said, smiling. Paul had already started working on the papers to get the divorce going.

Maria smiled and gave me a kiss. We both waited for the 'yuck', but it never came. I guess Crystal was happy that I was kissing someone who loved me and who I loved in return.

26

The next three and a half months were crazy. Detective Chambers was arrested and went to jail. Paul made sure the bail that was set for him was too high for him to afford to pay it. He also made sure he went to Greens where he didn't last two nights.

When he got there, they didn't put him into population because he was a cop, but they figured out a way to get to him anyway. The first day he was there, the guards mysteriously took him to the infirmary for an injury. Detective Chambers went willingly, thinking that he was getting some kind of special treatment.

The very next day while they were serving the food, someone stabbed him to death. They said that he was stabbed roughly forty times, which was the exact number of cases that was up for review because of suspected evidence tampering.

Crystal and I moved into Maria's house in Scottsdale. Maria stayed with us practically every day when we were at the hotel and Crystal loved her. She decided that Crystal's birthday present would be her very own room, painted in any color she desired. She said my Christmas present was a son – well, that was what she was hoping for when she found out she was pregnant.

She was still trying to get me to set a date for our wedding, but Emily refused to sign the divorce papers. I served them to her personally because she was still in town waiting on the assault trial, but she wouldn't sign them. She found out about Maria and me; she kept talking about how she would not give me a divorce so I could marry someone else.

Maria was arrested a couple of days after my meeting with Emily. Scott got an arrest warrant for her for aiding a wanted man. Paul quickly had the charges dropped, but Maria was still very upset for having been arrested in front of all of her co-workers. She lost all respect for the justice system, at least where we lived; but she kept her job as a detective. She said she had worked too hard just to throw all of it away.

Crystal started school after the Christmas vacation. She actually met up with some of her old friends from kindergarten. We had her records faxed in from California. I laughed when I read them. She had gotten into a fight with this little boy named Sean. She said that he talked about Emily and she let it go, then he talked about me and she punched him in his eye. The counselors at the new school warned her that things like that wouldn't be tolerated. I smiled at her and told her that I would just give her an half empty shower gel bottle every morning.

I also heard from Anthony. Some of his enemies had found out about his daughter. Anthony called Paul for help in getting his daughter to safety. Paul was going to bring Anthony's daughter to Scottsdale and hide her out, but Anthony didn't want her down here. He said that he had made more enemies in Greens than he did on the streets and he didn't want her anywhere near him.

Paul was working on a plan, but he wasn't moving fast enough. Anthony called and informed me that his enemies had gotten to his girl, his daughter's mother. They sent him pictures of them raping, torturing, and finally killing her. That was the first time in my life I have ever heard Anthony cry.

I told Maria the situation. She called a couple of friends that she had at the Bureau. They went to New York, found Anthony's daughter and put her into the Witness Protection Program. They changed her name and moved her to an outer part of Minnesota.

I told Anthony what happened. I told him that his daughter was safe and that his enemies shouldn't be looking for her because a news report in New York aired stating that she had been killed. Maria made sure that the report ran on every channel for a couple of days, so that whoever was looking for her had a chance to see it. Anthony cried again, his human side was returning to him also. He thanked Maria for everything and told her that if there was anything she ever needed, just to let him know.

The next day, Paul filed papers to get Anthony out of jail. With his daughter safe, he no longer had to stay in jail to protect her; and I knew he was coming out to go after the guys who did that stuff to his girl. I wanted to tell him what he had told me, to keep the animal inside; but after what his enemies had done, I knew it was the animal that was coming out of prison. After being with Maria and knowing how important she was to me while I was in prison, I would kill anyone who looked at her wrong - let alone raped, tortured, and then killed her!

I told Anthony that I would help him do what needed to be done, but he declined my help. He said that I had a family to take care of, and besides, he wanted to spill their blood himself. They had crossed the line, and they were about to feel his wrath.

The last three and a half months had flown past because a lot was going on. I thought that with spring around the corner, things would start to calm down, then I realized that my court date was only two weeks away.

Paul called me about a week before my trial to tell me that he had just received a call from Scott and that Emily wanted to meet with me. Paul strongly advised against meeting with her and even Maria was telling me not to go, but I had Paul arrange the meeting anyway. He arranged for the meeting on his turf at the hotel in Pineville in the room on the top floor. It was set up for nine o'clock at night.

Maria was a little over three months pregnant and was not at all happy with me meeting my wife in a hotel. I told her not to worry; I just wanted to see what she wanted and if I could get her to sign the divorce papers.

Maria said that if I slept with Emily, she would kill me. I would have laughed if I thought she was joking. I didn't laugh because it was obvious - she wasn't joking.

I tried to reassure her that I loved her and that she was the most beautiful woman in the world. I think that calmed her down for all of two seconds. She was stuck on the word hotel.

When I saw that sincerity wasn't working, I promised her that I would turn the shower on. She went into a mini rage, punching me in my arm and pinching whatever body fat she found on me. I knew her all too well. That was all that she needed to do, release her anger and frustration. Once she abused me, she felt a lot better about the meeting, but she still reminded me about the earlier threat that she would kill me.

I gave Crystal a hug and kiss and told her that I would be leaving for awhile and that she would have to stay with Maria. It would be the first time that I had left her since I was arrested for those forty-five minutes. She wanted to go with me, but I knew that I couldn't take her. Anything could happen and Emily could take her and I would never see her again.

Maria gave me one of her cell phones. She had three of them, two for work and one for personal. She gave me her personal cell phone and told me to call her if I needed anything. I gave her a kiss and headed out of the door.

I called Paul while I was in the car to make sure everything was set up. Paul confirmed that everything was done and all I needed to do was ask for the manager when I arrived. I started the car and headed towards the hotel, preparing to meet my wife.

27

I arrived at the hotel at nine o'clock that night. I walked in, got the keycard and went straight upstairs. The manager told me that Emily was already in the room waiting on me. I asked him if anyone came with her, trying to make sure that ten dudes weren't waiting for me in the room. He confirmed that she came alone and said that he watched her enter the room alone on the security camera. Paul really did set everything up.

I took the elevator up to the top floor. I walked into the room very quietly, seeing if I heard any voices. She was in the sitting area watching television.

"Well, it's about time," she said, turning the television off. She got up and walked over to me. She stood about ten feet from the door.

"Nice to see you, too," I said, closing the door. "What do you want?"

"You know what I want," she said.

I laughed and said, "Okay, what do you want that you can have? You know you are not getting Crystal back."

"She is my daughter, Jim. I gave birth to her. I carried her for nine months. She is my child and I am not leaving here until I get her back."

"Well, you won't be leaving then," I said. "I suggest you buy a house or rent an apartment or something, because she is never coming back to you."

"She is my child!" she said, raising her voice.

"So what?!" I said, raising my voice louder.

"I carried her!" she yelled back.

"SO WHAT! So what you carried her? You are nothing but a host anyway. You don't get special privileges because you carried her! You don't get points because you have a uterus. She is my daughter, always has been, always will be."

"Whatever, she came out of me," she said.

"She came out of me first," I replied.

We got quiet for a minute.

Emily tried to change up her approach because she saw that this was getting her nowhere. "Look, I am not here to fight you, but to offer you a deal."

"I'm listening," I said.

"I will sign the divorce papers and you can marry that Maria girl. I will also get Maurice to drop the charges from what happened at the restaurant if you give me Crystal back."

"Not happening," I said. "You can keep that deal."

"Look, I love Crystal and for the last six years while you were off doing whatever you were doing, I was raising her. I was taking care of her. Where were *you*?"

"I was in prison serving life for her *murder*. I was getting stabbed, beaten, choked, raped and everything else you can think of because they thought I killed her. For five and a half years, you were living in paradise and I was living in hell!"

Emily just stared at me, at a loss for words. She must not have realized all that I had been through for the last six years.

"She was with you for the last six years, wasn't she?"

"Yeah," she said, lowering her head.

"And you couldn't tell someone that she was alive? You couldn't visit me, write me or even tell the police that you had found her?"

"When I found her I came back to the house to get you, but you were gone. I didn't know who took her, so I was scared to tell anyone.

I was scared that they might try to take her again. I thought you left, so I tried to get as far away from Scottsdale as possible."

"So you went to California," I said.

"Yeah, California."

"Is that where you met Maurice?"

"No, he was from here. He helped me to get out of here when I couldn't find you. He found us a place out there and stayed with us. He really loves Crystal, Jim. You should give him a chance."

"Was that the same guy who said that she ran away? And you where the same person said you wish, right? You call that love?"

"Jim, that was taken out of context. We were joking about something in the car before we even got to the restaurant. We were just continuing the joke. I admit it was in bad taste, but it was only a joke."

I walked into the sitting room and sat down on the couch. I grabbed her pocket book that was sitting on the couch. It fell over when I sat down and all of her stuff spilled onto the couch. I stuffed everything back into the pocketbook and sat it on the coffee table.

"I thank you for taking care of Crystal for so long, but there is no way that I am giving her up."

"Well, that is just not acceptable," she said as she walked over to the chair. She sat down, crossed her legs and stared at me.

"Look, I am not trying to be here all night," I said. "There is no way that I'm giving up Crystal. We can go around and around, but that fact is not going to change."

"I am not asking you to give up Crystal. I just said that I am not leaving here without her."

I looked at her confused and asked, "What are you saying?"

"Come back to California with me. You have the money to do it, and we can all be together," she said.

"What? Maria is not going to want to move to California."

"I didn't invite Maria. I invited my husband and my daughter to California, not her."

I laughed and questioned, "And what about Maurice?"

"He knows that I am married and that I love my husband. He knows how committed I am to my family and you are my family, Jim."

I shook my head in utter amazement. I just couldn't believe that she was sitting here saying all of these things.

"I am sorry, but it's not going to happen, I….."

Before I could finish speaking, she cut me off, "Jim, we are in a wonderful hotel room. Why don't we enjoy each other's company? I could put on something a little more comfortable, and we could really have some fun."

"Why do you want to have fun with me?" I asked.

She looked at me, confused.

"You didn't want to have fun with me when we were married and lived together, why would you want to do it now?"

"I haven't seen you in years. I missed you, Jim. Did you forget how much I love you?"

"I must have, but I didn't forget that you stopped being bothered with me for a year and some change before Crystal was kidnapped. I didn't forget that we didn't even sleep in the same bed for months at a time. I didn't forget that you worked all the time, even when we had plans and were supposed to do stuff as a family. So, please remind me of this love that you had or have for me."

Emily got up, walked over to me and tried to kiss me, but I turned my head away. She took a couple of steps back and asked, "So, you don't want to kiss me?"

I didn't even answer that question. I just stared at her.

She smiled and said, "Well, let's see if you want to kiss me after you see me in this." She held up a pair of white panties and a sheer silk robe that appeared to go with them.

She grabbed her pocketbook, walked into the bathroom and closed the door. I shook my head for a moment and then got up to leave. There was no way I was going to be with her. First of all, I could never do that to Maria after all that she had done for me. Second, something just wasn't right, Emily was being too nice. She had never been like that to me in her life, even in our good times together. Third and most importantly, Maria would kill me, literally. I had just gotten Crystal back and I was not about to get killed by my baby's mother for sleeping with my wife, as crazy as that sounded. I laughed to myself as I approached the door. If that wasn't the greatest talk show topic of all time, then I didn't know what was. I could picture it now, everyone in the audience booing Maria because she was the girlfriend and Emily on the stage crying because she missed me so much. That would be hilarious.

Before I reached the door, I heard a cell phone ring. I pulled the cell phone out of my pocket to answer it, but it wasn't ringing. I followed the music back to the couch. I moved the cushion and saw that there was a phone in between the cushion and the couch. It must have been Emily's phone. It must have fallen inside the couch cushions when I had knocked her pocketbook over.

The phone had stopped ringing. I flipped it open to see who had called her and a messaged popped up to tell her she missed a call. I clicked the okay button to see if I could see a number… no number, just a name - Scott.

"Scott," I said to myself. "What in the world was Scott doing calling her?" I started to go through her phone. I checked her contacts. Scott's name and phone number were programmed into her phone. I checked the date that it was programmed. It read that it was entered on November 14, 2005.

"2005," I thought out loud. That was a couple of months before Crystal was kidnapped. Anger filled me quickly. If Emily knew Scott, then she knew about everything that had happened.

Just then, she walked out of the bathroom with the silk robe and white panties on. She spun around slowly to show me the whole package.

She walked over to me and as she was about to put her arms around me, I spoke. "You know Scott."

She paused and replied, "Huh. I'm sorry, I don't know a Scott."

"That is funny," I said, "because he just called you." I held up the cell phone for her to see it.

She looked stunned for a minute. "Wait a minute, my cell phone is in my pocketbook, that can't be mine."

She walked back into the bathroom and looked through her pocketbook for a minute. "See, it's right here," she shouted from the bathroom.

She came out of the bathroom, walked back over to me and said, "Where were we?"

"Let me see your cell phone," I demanded.

"Why?" she replied.

"Because I want to see it."

She just stood there and looked at me, not knowing what to say.

"Well, where is your cell phone?" I asked.

"It's in the bathroom," she said.

"Stop lying."

"It is in the bathroom."

"Stop lying!" I shouted. "Your phone is right here in my hand. How do you know Scott?"

She saw that there was no way she was going to lie her way out of it. She said, "He is a friend of Maurice."

Everything started to add up. "You lying ho," I said as the anger started to build up inside me. "You knew Scott before Crystal was kidnapped. You knew about everything that happened. You knew that I was in jail."

She walked over to me and tried to hug me.

"Get off of me," I said, pushing her arms back. "Don't ever touch me!"

"Jim, I am sorry," she said, trying to make her eyes water up.

"Sorry.......sorry? You are sorry! Do you have any idea what I went through because of you? Do you have any idea the torture that I went through, the pain and suffering that I went through? You are sorry?" I asked, as I looked at her in disgust.

"Well, what do you want me to say?" she asked me.

"There is nothing that you can say. You are just unbelievable. You put me through all of that, for what? Just tell me for what."

"There really isn't an answer for that."

"There better be an answer. I know I just didn't lose six years of my life because it was just something for you to do. I know you didn't put Crystal through all of that just because it was fun....."

"No," she interrupted. "I couldn't be with Maurice and have Crystal because I knew she would never leave you. So we thought of a way to try to get Crystal. I am sorry that everything happened the way that it did. I never meant for you to get hurt."

Rage entered my body as I said, "You did all of this for a man, a man that you were cheating on me with. You are so stupid. I can't believe this." I was so pissed off that I didn't know what to say. "And you didn't want Crystal anyway; that is why you were stepping out on her and me."

Emily went back into the bathroom, grabbed her clothes and started to get dressed. She threw on her clothes and ran back out of the bathroom.

"What do you mean that I didn't want Crystal? She is my first child. I will always love her and I have always wanted her."

"That is garbage. You would leave her to go be with Maurice, so how are you going to say you wanted her?"

"I wanted her, I just didn't want you!" she yelled.

"I had nothing to do with her, and that is a sad excuse to run out on your child."

"You had everything to do with her. She was you. She walked like you. She talked like you. She looked exactly like you. She is a younger version of you."

It finally clicked into my brain. "You hated the fact that she didn't want you, and you hated me for it. You were jealous of your own daughter, you sorry excuse for a mother!"

"You don't know what it's like to be the outsider in your own home."

"Don't try to pull that 'feel sorry for me' crap. You made yourself the outsider when you decided to leave the home."

"You just wouldn't understand."

"You're right, I wouldn't," I said. "I wouldn't understand how a mother could be jealous of the relationship between a father and daughter. I just wouldn't understand that."

I turned around to leave. I had had enough of this conversation.

"Where are you going?" Emily questioned.

"Back home to my real wife," I retorted.

"Your real wife is here," she said, grabbing my arm.

"Let me explain something to you. First, you are not my real wife. You are nothing to me. Second, the only reason I have not put my fist through your forehead is because of my daughter and my real wife." I snatched my arm away from her. "And as I said to you before, do not touch me."

She ran around me and stood between me and the door. "You are not going anywhere."

I laughed to myself and thought, *Whoever was supposed to send out the memo on me is fired, because NO ONE has gotten it.* I tried to go around her, but she wouldn't move.

"Emily, can you please get out of the way so that I can go?"

"No, you are not leaving here. And what do you mean 'you haven't put your fist through my forehead'? I know you don't think that you can hit me. You must have forgotten who you married. I'm not that little Spanish chick you're messing with. I will fight you back."

She was just trying to start an argument. I have been here too many times before with her. All she wanted to do was fuss, and I didn't have time for that.

"Move," I said.

"Make me," she replied.

She was trying me and my patience; but for whatever reason, I just couldn't bring myself to hit her.

Then all of a sudden, her cell phone beeped. I flipped it open. She had a text message from Scott. She ran over to me to try to get the phone out of my hand. I held her back with my left hand as I read the message from Scott from the phone in my right hand.

The message read:

> *Keep him at the hotel.*
> *We are almost to the house.*

I finished reading the message, closed the phone and turned to her.

"What house are they going to?" I asked, balling up my fist in anger.

"Don't worry about it," she said, backing up a little bit.

I walked towards her and asked more forcefully, "What house are they going to?"

"What? What are you going to do?" she asked, looking at my fist. "Please little boy, I wish you would."

Wish granted. I dropped the phone out of my hand and punched her directly in the mouth. She fell back into the table by the door and then onto the floor. Blood instantly flowed from her mouth. She tried to get up, but she was too dizzy to do it.

"What house are they going to?"

"Don't worry about it!"

I kicked her in her stomach as hard as humanly possible. She curled up in the fetal position, in pain. She screamed for help, but I bent down and grabbed her around the throat before anyone could hear her. I squeezed on her throat just enough to cut off the oxygen for five seconds and let it go so she could talk.

"What house are they going to?" I screamed. I knew, but I just wanted her to say it.

"Is that the best you got? My son hits harder than you and he isn't even three yet," she said, still bent over on the ground in pain.

"If you want hard, you got it."

I cocked back and punched her in the jaw, causing her head to smack the hardwood floor again. She started crying as the pain caught up with her.

She tried to crawl away, but I grabbed her foot. She started kicking wildly, trying to get me off of her. I let her leg go, walked in to the sitting area, grabbed a chair and threw it on her. The chair crashed into her back, bounced, hit her in the head and rolled against the door. She stopped crawling; the pain was too much.

"You are nothing but a hooker. They made you come here to sleep with me so that they could try to get Crystal. You thought you could set me up," I said, kicking her in the ribs. "You thought I was going to trust you after all you did," I said, kicking her in the back.

"Please stop. I am sorry," she said, trying to put her hands up.

I laughed and said, "Stop? I am just getting started."

I picked her up and stood her on her feet. She grabbed onto me to hold her balance. I straightened her up so that she could stand up. As soon as she gained her balance, I punched her in the mouth, knocking her back down to the floor. My mind had snapped and it wasn't coming back.

I stomped on her stomach and shouted, "That is for every fight I had!" She curled up to try to protect herself. I kicked her as hard as I could in her thigh and yelled, "That is for every night I spent in prison!" Tears flowed down her face and blood poured from her mouth. She laid on her side on the floor. I grabbed the table by the door and slammed it on her as hard as I could. "That is for every time I got stabbed!" I picked her up by her hair as she tried to scream for help, but just as she opened her mouth, I clasped my hand around her throat.

"Scream. I want you to. Come on, scream!" I said as I continued to choke her.

She grabbed my arm and dug her nails into it. I picked her up and threw her across the room. She hit the side of the couch and fell on the floor.

She picked herself up and put her hands up.

"Come on!" she yelled.

I laughed and asked, "Are you serious?" If she did that to give herself courage or to make herself feel strong, she should've tried something else because all it did was piss me off more.

I walked up to her and she started to swing at me wildly, just throwing her hands in every direction. She smacked and punched me a couple of times, but really only managed to make me angrier.

I punched her in the chest right between her breasts, knocking all of the oxygen out of her body and putting an end to her fighting effort. She fell to the floor, trying to breathe. I just smiled as I opened up my hand and smacked her across the face.

She tried to plead with me. "Please, just stop. Just leave me alone."

"I went through five and a half years, and you think I am going to be finished after five and a half minutes?"

She was on the floor on her hands and knees. I kicked her again, this time trying to break her ribs. She fell back onto the floor with tears running down her face. The pain and agony that was present on her face made my blood rush. It was like the sight of a beautiful woman to a lonely man; it made my heart beat faster.

I picked her head up and punched her on the right side of her face close to her eye. Her head flew back to the ground. I picked her head up again and punched her on the left side of her face, making her head fly back to the ground harder.

She tried to kick me, but her attempts were weak at best. The beating had taken its toll on her and she no longer had the ability to fight back. I caught her foot in mid-air, and twisted her ankle until I heard it pop. The pain shot through her body and she let out a monstrous scream. The only problem for her was that we were in the only room on the top floor; no one could hear her.

She crawled away again. I walked slowly behind her, watching her struggle. She made it to the patio door before she finally lost the energy to continue. She fell to the ground and tried to rest.

I bent down beside her and whispered, "I have to go play with your friend now. You make sure to be a good little girl, okay?" I stood up and walked away. Before I got to the door, I heard her laughing. I turned around to see her on the floor with her back against the door, facing me.

"You are too late. Maurice should have Crystal by now and be headed back to California. All I had to do was keep you here," she said, laughing. "And you were stupid enough to stay."

That is the one thing that I have always loved about a woman; they never know when to shut up.

I walked over to her. I gently ran my hand through her hair, grabbed a handful and banged her head against the glass repeatedly. She screamed as the glass cracked and blood began to appear.

"Hey, I have an idea! Maybe they are going to fly back to California… and here's a thought, you can fly with them!"

I picked her up and banged her into the balcony door. After the third time, she went straight through, breaking the glass. She crawled backwards, keeping her eyes on me while trying to get away.

I picked up the patio chair and threw it at her as hard as I could. She tried to block it with her hand, but it was thrown with too much force. The leg of the chair hit three of her fingers and bent them back, breaking two of them.

I went over to pick her up and throw her over the rail, but as I walked up to her I heard her cell phone ring.

"I'll be right back, honey." I walked back into the room and picked up her cell phone. I opened it and read the message.

We are at the house.
Going in to get her.

I walked back onto the balcony and kicked her in the mouth, knocking out four of her teeth. "I have to go now. Maybe we can do this some other time."

I ran out of the room and took the elevator downstairs. As I was leaving the hotel, I called Paul. He answered the phone and knew it was me.

"How did it go?" he asked.

"You have to take care of it," I said.

"What happened? What did you do?"

"She is lying on the balcony, near death. She set me up Paul. She set me up!"

"What do you need me to do?" he asked.

"The top floor is a mess. You have to get it cleaned up. You have to get everything cleaned up."

"You were never there," he said.

"Paul, I don't want to know, just do what you do," I said as I got into the car.

"You got it. Where are you going now?"

"Home. I have to go make sure they don't take Crystal."

"Call me if you need me," Paul said.

"You know I will," I said.

We hung up the phone and I called Maria, but she didn't answer the phone. I just hoped that I wasn't too late. I couldn't take losing Crystal again, especially not like this.

28

I drove as fast as I could to get home. I had taken Emily's cell phone, just in case they sent another message.

As I pulled onto the street to get to my house, her cell phone rang. I flipped it opened to receive the text message, which said:

We have her.

I sped up and raced down the street. I pulled up just in time to see Scott standing in the front yard and Maurice pulling Crystal by her arm towards the car. Maria was laying in the grass, curled up.

I parked the car directly behind theirs, blocking it from leaving the driveway. I jumped out of the car and slammed the door.

Scott turned to me and said, "Now look, don't you do anything stupid."

"Stupid?" I asked as I walked to the trunk of my car. I popped the trunk and grabbed the baseball bat that I kept inside for special occasions like this.

"Hey, you better remember who I am."

I laughed a little and said, "Yeah, I remember who you are."

My anger had reached an all time high. I was boiling hot - hotter than my anger for the inmates in prison, for the people who spat in my food, even for the guards who took Crystal's picture. For the first time since Crystal told me, I felt what she had seen in her dream. The animal inside of me was loose again.

I walked up to Scott as he tried to stand before me as if he was fearless. Maurice had stopped trying to pull Crystal and just stood there with her, holding her.

Maria screamed at me, "Jim! Jim!"

Crystal looked at her and calmly spoke, "That is not him. Look at his eyes, he is gone."

Just as she said that, the sound of the bat cracking against Scott's head echoed throughout the neighborhood. Blood flew everywhere as I repeatedly hit him with the baseball bat. He screamed, but there was no stopping me. I hit him until he stopped screaming, stopped moving, stopped breathing.

Maurice just stood there, terrified. I began to walk towards him. He screamed at me.

"Get away from us," he yelled and wrapped his arms around Crystal tightly.

"Let me go!" Crystal screamed.

"You heard her, let her go," I said.

"Look, I don't want any more trouble. Just let me take my daughter and get out of here," he said.

My anger went higher.

"Your daughter!? Your daughter!?"

I dropped the bat, ran over to him and tried to separate him from Crystal. I was going to swing the bat at him, he was so cowardly that he would have turned Crystal towards me and made me hit her. I decided to choke him. I grabbed him around the throat and proceeded to choke him. He held on to Crystal as long as he could, but with his oxygen cut off and Crystal steadily fighting him, she was able to break away. Once Crystal ran away, it was just Maurice and I. He had already expended a lot of energy just trying to hang on to Crystal, so he was too weak to try to get my arm from around his throat. We struggled for a couple of seconds and I finally let him go. He dropped to the ground and coughed heavily. I picked up the bat and swung as hard as I could, hitting him in the back of the head. He fell flat on the ground looking paralyzed. I kept hitting him. Blow after blow brought more and more blood.

Crystal ran over to Maria and tried to help her up. Maria got up off the ground and walked towards me.

"Honey, I think that he is dead," she said. Police sirens started to sing in the night.

Maria had on a pair of light blue pajama pants. Well, they had started off light blue. As she walked towards me, I noticed that the pants were dark in between her legs, and getting darker by the second.

"Maria, are you okay?" I said as I looked down at her pants.

Maria looked down and began to cry. "I don't know," she said through tears.

Just then, the police pulled up and jumped out of the car. I screamed at them to call the paramedics as I ran over to Maria. She wrapped her arm around me.

The policeman called it in on his radio, "Officer injured. I repeat, Officer injured. We need a paramedic unit stat."

The paramedics arrived in about three minutes and took her to the hospital. Maria was fine, but the baby didn't make it. She told me that Scott and Maurice broke into the house while I was gone. When she tried to protect Crystal, Maurice pushed her into the wall and she fell on the floor hard.

Maria apologized to me thousands of times. She said that she should have just gotten her gun and shot them, or been smart and hidden Crystal, then the baby would be here today. She felt terrible because she knew how much I was looking forward to the baby, and she really wanted to have it.

I apologized to her also. I felt like it was my fault that the baby wouldn't be here. If I wasn't beating the life out of Emily and had left when I knew what was happening, I would have been there to protect them.

Crystal kept apologizing too, which broke both of our hearts. She felt that if she weren't there, then her little brother would still be alive. All of our hearts were broken, but the love that we had for each other pulled us through.

29

Two weeks had passed since that night. My case regarding the attack in the restaurant parking lot was postponed due to the prosecution and the victim getting killed. The next day, the State dropped the case. They tried to find Emily, but she had fled with her son back to California. They were unable to find her.

There were no charges brought against me for that night either. Emily didn't press charges regarding the hotel beating; she just left and went into hiding. Maurice and Scott were both found to be in the wrong. Breaking and entering, attempted kidnapping, assault on a police officer, assault on a pregnant woman - they pretty much signed their death notices when they came to the house. I would have been justified to kill them if they had committed just one of these crimes, so the State labeled the case self-defense and closed it.

After two weeks of misery, Maria decided to get out of the house for the day. She left early in the morning after dropping Crystal off at school. She used Emily's cell phone to find Maurice's mother. She called her a couple of days earlier and arranged a meeting with her at her house. She arranged the meeting as a Detective looking for information. His mother was more than willing to meet.

She pulled up and knocked on the door. His mother answered the door, introduced herself as Glenda and welcomed Detective Diaz into her home.

They sat down at the table and Maria began with her questions.

"Glenda, I first want to thank you so much for meeting with me."

"Oh, that is not a problem, darling. Would you like some coffee or something?"

"No, thank you ma'am. I just have a couple of questions and then I will be out of your way."

"Well, okay. Ask your questions," Glenda said.

"Have you ever met a lady named Emily?" Maria asked.

"Emily, yes I met her before. That was Maurice's girlfriend," Glenda said sadly. The fact that she had just buried her son still weighed heavily on her heart.

"Okay," Maria said. "Do you remember when you first met her?"

"Oh," Glenda said as she thought about it. "It was about twelve years ago. He brought her over the house and told me that she was pregnant. He said that she was having his baby and that he was going to marry her. She already had a wedding ring on, so I knew she was already married."

"So, he thought that she was pregnant with his baby?" Maria asked. She was trying to make sure she heard Glenda correctly.

"That is what Emily must have told him, because he kept going on and on about what he was going to name it. He even made me go shopping and buy baby clothes for it."

Maria just looked at Glenda and tried to keep a straight face. Underneath the face was sorrow for Maurice and pure hatred for Emily. She hated her for what she did to the both of us.

"How did Emily meet Maurice?"

"He told me that they met in a bar. He was in law school and he went out with his buddy Scott one night for drink, and….."

Maria cut her off, "Scott Benson, the lawyer who was killed the other night?"

Glenda lowered her head and replied, "Yeah, that was the same Scott. They went to school together. They went in different fields with Scott into criminal and Maurice into tax law, but they were the best of friends."

The pieces of the puzzle were coming together. That was how Emily and Maurice knew Scott. Maria got ready to ask her next question.

"Miss Glenda, have you ever seen Crystal?"

"Oh yeah, child. Emily brought Crystal over a couple of times when she was a baby. I didn't see her for years after that and then one day, Emily showed up with Crystal in a robe and asked me to watch her. She said that Maurice was going to be over to pick her up in a couple of days."

"In a robe? Didn't that seem a little strange?" Maria asked.

"Yes it did, but she looked like she was in trouble so I didn't want to make the situation worse by asking questions. Besides, it was freezing outside and all she had on was a robe."

"And when did this happen?" questioned Maria.

"Oh, about six years ago."

Instantly Maria realized that was the day that Crystal had been kidnapped. Maria felt anger beyond description, but she had to keep a calm demeanor because she didn't want to scare Glenda. She had a lot more questions now and they weren't going to get answered if Glenda clammed up.

Maria breathed deeply to try to release some anger. She continued, "So Crystal stayed here for a couple of days?"

"Yeah, about a week, then Maurice and Emily came and picked her up. I really don't remember, but I do remember that she was sad the whole time she was here. She kept talking about her daddy. She missed him very much. I kept telling her that he was going to come to pick her up and that would cheer her up for a couple of minutes, but then she would go back to feeling sad. There was nothing that I could do for her."

Glenda got up and walked to the sink. She filled up a glass with water, grabbed a pill bottle and sat back down at the table.

"I'm sorry, but I have to take my medication."

"That is no problem at all. If you want, we can do this later," Maria said. She really didn't want to stop, but she was trying to be considerate to Glenda. She was trying to show her that she cared, even if she had to pretend to do it.

"No, I am fine. Just need to pop of couple of pills and I am right as rain." Glenda took her medication and began to speak again.

"You know, between you and me, I knew that Crystal wasn't his child."

"You did?" Maria asked. "How?"

"Well for one, she looked nothing like him. I mean she didn't even have his ears. Everyone in our family has those ears, but she didn't. And she didn't know him. Every time I would say his name, she would act like I was talking about a total stranger. That little girl wasn't his child. I just knew it."

Maria wrote some notes down on her paper. She did this to make it look like she was conducting an official investigation into Maurice's death. She was conducting an investigation, but it wasn't official. It was her personal investigation that had just gotten a lot more interesting.

"Did you tell Maurice about your doubts of Crystal being his child?"

"He knew, but I don't think that he wanted to face it. He would talk to me all the time about Emily, Crystal and Emily's husband. As a matter of fact, he called me a couple of days before Emily showed up that day. He said that he talked with Emily and gave her a choice. She either had to leave her husband and bring his daughter, or he was going to move to California and cut her off completely."

"California?" Maria asked.

"Yes ma'am, California. His job was transferring him out there."

"So then a couple of days later, she showed up with Crystal on your doorstep."

"Yes she did, in the middle of winter with nothing but a robe on."

"From the police report, she didn't have a car to drive. How did she manage to get Crystal over here?" Maria asked.

"Oh, Maurice let her use his car. He had a gray car that he would let her drive from time to time."

Maria sat for a second and tried to gather her thoughts. "Why do you think that after seven years of being married to a man Emily would get up and run off to California with your son?"

"Money," Glenda said without even thinking about the answer. "And my son was a fine looking man."

Maria laughed her to herself. *Not anymore*, she thought. She caught herself and felt bad, thinking that she was getting as bad as me.

Glenda continued, "But that is not why she would leave her husband. Maurice was going to be somebody. He had money. He had friends. He had the life that Emily wanted, and she was not about to let him go."

"Did you tell Maurice that?"

"Child, he knew, but he wanted her just as bad as she wanted him. I don't know what he wanted her for, but he did. No matter what I said or did, that fact didn't change."

Maria decided to go back to Crystal. "Did you know that Crystal was reported kidnapped six years ago?"

"You know, I recall seeing something like that on television. I told Maurice, but he said that they must have been talking about another Crystal, not his Crystal. They showed the picture and everything. I knew that was her, but he kept saying that little girl wasn't her, so I left it alone."

Maria's anger got the best of her.

"You left it alone? Jim Sutton spent over five years in prison for the kidnapping and murder of Crystal Sutton, and you didn't think to contact the police about the little girl you knew your son had."

Glenda felt attacked, but she knew that she was wrong. "I am sorry, I didn't want to get involved."

Maria's tempter still flared as she exclaimed, "Get involved, you practically helped them kidnap the child!"

Glenda became defensive and retorted, "I did no such thing! The child's mother asked me to watch the child. That was all I did!"

Maria tried to calm down. She still needed information from Glenda, but it was too late.

"I think it is about time you left," Glenda said as she got up from the table and walked to the door.

Maria followed and said, "Thank you so much for your time."

Glenda didn't say anything. She just quickly shut the door as soon as Maria walked out.

Maria walked to the car, got in and started driving home. She began to put the pieces of the puzzle together and called me on her cell phone.

"Hello," I said, picking up the cordless phone.

"Hey baby, got a minute?" she asked.

"Sure, is this serious? Do I need to be alone?"

"Yeah, I think you do."

I excused myself from Crystal and our never ending game of I DECLARE WAR. We were playing poker and betting cookies, but she kept beating me. So I changed up the game and we ate the rest of the cookies.

Maria's house was huge. I walked upstairs into the bedroom and left Crystal downstairs in the living room. I turned up the television in the living room just in case my conversation with Maria got loud. I figured that she was going to say something that might upset me because she told me to be alone. Crystal had seen and heard enough of that for a lifetime. I was trying to avoid her having to hear it again.

"What's up?" I said as I shut the door.

"Guess who I just had a meeting with?"

"A therapist. You finally believe what I was saying about you being crazy and you went to get help."

"No. Glenda, Maurice's mother…. and I will punch you for that one later."

I laughed and said, "Okay. Well, what did she have to say?"

"You might want to sit down for this."

I laid across the bed and said, "I am laying down, go ahead."

"Are you ready?" Maria said, pulling the car to the side of the road.

"Yeah."

"She told me that Emily was messing with Maurice for about a year before Crystal was born. Emily told Maurice that Crystal was his child. When Maurice finally got tired of not seeing 'his child', he gave Emily an ultimatum. She had to get Crystal and move with him to California, or he would leave her for good."

"And she chose California," I said, putting the puzzle together myself.

"Exactly," she said. "She used Maurice's car to come home that morning and grab Crystal. She didn't have time to get her dressed, so she threw a robe on her and took her to Maurice's mother. Crystal stayed there for about a week, then Emily and Maurice came to get her."

"I should have killed her," slipped out of my mouth. At that very second, I wished for one more punch, one more kick. I wished I could have gotten another twenty seconds and threw her over the balcony; but if I had, Crystal would probably be gone and it wouldn't have been worth it. That still didn't change the fact that I wished that I would have tossed her, though.

"What? What happened with the meeting that night anyway?"

"Nothing important, we can talk about that later. What else did she say?"

"That Maurice and Scott have known each other for a long time and even went to law school together. Emily chose Maurice because of his money and social status and because Maurice was a fine looking man."

I chuckled and interjected, "Not anymore."

Maria laughed and admitted, "That was the same thing I said to myself."

"Well, are you okay?" I asked.

"I am fine," Maria said. "The question is, are you okay?"

"No, but I will be. I have an eleven year old daughter downstairs beating me to death in cards. I don't have time to worry about the past. Besides, my girlfriend would kill me if I sat back and worried about my wife."

"You better rephrase that because I am your wife. I don't care what that piece of paper says," Maria said. I could just picture her in the car going off on the cell phone.

"I know baby, you are my wife."

"You better know," she replied.

I breathed for a second to try to shake off the last conversation.

"Where are you now?" I asked.

"Sitting on the side of the road," she said. "I have to take care of one more thing before I come home."

"Okay, tell your boyfriend I said 'hi'."

She laughed and joked, "Why do you do that? Don't you know I would never tell him about you?"

I smirked and asked playfully, "You know I would kill both of you, right?"

"Yeah, I know. But you should know I love you too much to ever do anything like that."

"Yeah, I know. What do you want for dinner tonight?" I asked.

"I will cook when I get home, don't worry about that. I will see you in a couple of hours."

We got off the phone and I went back downstairs. Crystal and I played cards, cooked something to eat and watched television until Maria got home.

That night, Maria cooked a special Spanish dish that was fabulous. We sat around and ate together. Maria was especially nice that night. I think the reality of what we went through had smacked her again, and she was just trying to show us that she loved us and no one else.

30

Two weeks later, there was a knock at the door as we were about to leave the house to go to breakfast.

As I walked to the door, I shouted, "Who is it?"

"Open the door and find out!" someone shouted back.

I recognized the voice immediately. "Well, I don't know if you know, but this is a police officer's house. So if you happen to be a criminal, then you might want to leave."

"Good thing I am not a criminal."

My spirit was high as I opened the door. "What in Sam Hill are you doing here?" I asked. I grabbed the man and hugged him.

"I had some business that I had to take care of," he replied.

Maria came walking out of the kitchen with Crystal just as he walked into the house and I closed the door. I walked over to Maria and Crystal, hugged them both and introduced them to my visitor.

"Maria and Crystal, this is the man who kept me alive in prison. Anthony, this is my girlfriend Maria.....," she punched me in the arm. "I meant to say wife! This little lady right here is the reason why I live."

Anthony walked up to Maria and gave her a hug and a kiss on the cheek.

"Are you taking care of my man for me?"

"Yeah, I am trying to," Maria said, kissing him on the cheek.

He stared at Crystal for a minute, speechless. He didn't know what to say, or at least didn't have the right words to say. Finally he spoke, "Do you know how much your daddy loves you?"

Crystal smiled and said, "Yes."

He hugged her and she hugged him back.

"Thank you for helping my daddy," Crystal said.

Anthony's eyes welled up. I knew his heart was like stone, but Crystal had a way of softening any heart. He quickly wiped his eyes with his hands, trying to hide the emotion.

"Oh man, do you want something to drink or something?" I asked.

"I'm alright. I just stopped past to give you something."

Maria told Crystal to go into the living room and watch television because we had to talk for a minute. Crystal gave Anthony another hug and walked into the living room. We went into the basement to try to get a little privacy. Whatever reason Anthony came for, Maria didn't want Crystal to hear it.

Once we were settled in the basement with Maria and I on the couch and Anthony in a chair, he started to pull things out of a black bag that he had been carrying. He handed me disc after disc, until finally I asked. "What are all of these?"

"These are your wedding presents from me."

"Wedding presents?" I asked. Maria just looked at me and smiled.

"Oh yeah, and congratulations on your divorce," Anthony said as he smiled and winked at Maria.

"Okay, what happened?" I asked.

"Nothing," he said and shook his head. "It is just official, you are divorced."

"She signed the papers?" I asked.

"Not exactly. Let's just say that you got the other, less expensive divorce."

I stopped breathing for a second because I knew what he was talking about. "How did you find her?"

"I have my connections, you know that."

"She was in California?" I asked.

"Yeah."

"And the son?" I questioned.

"No witnesses, no survivors."

I felt bad for a second. Not for Emily because she deserved to die ten times over, but for the little boy. He just was born to the wrong woman. He did nothing wrong but survive the birth.

"Why? Didn't you have other business to take care of? How did that become a priority?" He knew I wasn't asking out of anger, but just pure curiosity.

"Well, I got a call from a mutual friend of ours. He said that a young woman came to see him and told him that she wanted to get married. He told her to get married. She said that she couldn't and told him about a little problem she was having in California. So, I went to California to take care of the problem for the young woman."

I looked at Maria, but she wouldn't look at me. She kept staring at Anthony, purposely trying not to make eye contact with me. I punched her softly in her leg and she burst out laughing.

"What was that for?" she said as she grabbed the spot where I hit her.

I began to mock her. "I can't believe you." Slapping her in her face softly, I said, "You make me so angry."

She laughed as she covered up her face. "I don't care if you think it was right or wrong, I just want you to understand," she said, repeating what I told her.

I shook my head and look back at Anthony. "Was it quick?"

"Five shots apiece, one for every year."

I paused for a minute and tried to collect my thoughts. I looked down at the discs and asked, "What are these?"

"These, my friend, are home movies of a little girl that I believe you know."

I was still trying to pull it together. I really didn't feel sorry for Emily and her son, but I felt like I was supposed to. I felt like any person who had any feelings or emotions at all would feel - just the tiniest amount of remorse or pity. No matter how hard I thought, I just couldn't feel anything for them. So after thirty seconds of trying, I gave up.

"I am surrounded by a bunch of killers," I said, laughing. I picked up a pillow and threw it at Maria. "And you are a cop," I added.

She caught the pillow, laughed and replied, "I never said to kill anyone. All I told this mutual friend was that I wanted to get married and I asked him politely to take care of it. It appears that he did. Thank you Anthony."

"No, thank you. I owe you so much more. You gave me my life back and protected my daughter. I would have done it for nothing."

"Oh, that is not a problem," Maria said, smiling. "You protected my baby, so I protected yours," she said as she rubbed the back of my neck.

"Freaking murdering ......," I said, looking at both of them.

Anthony smiled and said, "Man, you have killed more people than I have. Let me tell you about your man, Maria."

I cut in, "That's okay. We can save that conversation for another day."

"No, no, I want to hear this," Maria said.

I looked at Anthony and shook my head no. Maria had lost it when she found out about the guards. I really didn't think she could take half of the stuff that I did in prison. Besides, I didn't want Anthony to speak about it like he was bragging or boasting because that life contained nothing to brag or boast about.

"Maria, that man saved my life too many times. He is truly a wonderful human being," Anthony said.

Maria punched me in my arm. "What are you hiding?"

I laughed and said, "Nothing. That man told you what he had to tell you." I quickly changed the subject. "So, are you finished handling all of your business?"

"Yeah. I have a little more to finish up, but other than that, I'm done."

"How is your daughter?" Maria asked.

"She is wonderful, thank you." Anthony said.

"So she was happy to see you?" I asked.

"Believe it or not, she really was. Her mother told her about me, but she never badmouthed me. She told her every day how much I loved her and how I had to go away for her protection."

"So, her mother knew you were hiding?" I asked.

"Yeah, she knew. She was a smart one. I really never could hide things from her," Anthony said, pausing to remember his love.

"How is your daughter doing, son?" Anthony asked.

"Wonderful, just wonderful," I said. I grabbed and held Maria's hand. "She has a mother who loves her and a daddy who would kill anyone to protect her."

We talked for a little bit more, then Anthony had to leave. He gave me all of his contact information. He was going to be staying in Minnesota with his daughter.

We went out to breakfast and rushed home because I wanted to see the home movies. I set up in the living room to watch the DVDs that Anthony had brought. Maria took Crystal out of the house for awhile. She didn't want her to know that we had them. I popped in the first one, sat down on the couch and hit play.

A lady appeared on a microphone. She was standing in front of a stage, introducing the children as they walked down the cafeteria. Anger flared up when I saw Crystal. She was beautiful, but she was so sad walking down the aisle. It angered me that I wasn't there, that Emily had robbed me of that moment. Crystal looked beautiful in her dress, but she didn't enjoy her kindergarten graduation. I could tell by her eyes that she missed me. I could tell by her attitude that she was looking for me.

I forced myself to continue to watch. Tears began to drop from my eyes as I saw her stand there, helpless. I heard Emily in the background screaming, "Smile!"

She whispered to whoever was holding the camera, "She needs more medication," and laughed. I am assuming that it was Maurice beside her.

He laughed, "She needs more than medication."

Both of them laughed as he struggled to hold the camera straight. As they were laughing it up, Crystal's name was called. No one cheered for her. No one clapped. She just received her paper and walked back to her place in line.

I stopped the tape. I couldn't take it. I wished that they were alive right now, just so I could have the pleasure of killing them. That was her graduation and they had stolen it from me and ruined it for Crystal.

I tried to watch a couple more of the discs, but was forced to turn them off. All of them were the same; Crystal looking or acting miserable, and Emily and Maurice making fun of her or just not dealing with her.

As she got older, the movies showed her holding or caring for her little brother, and the only reason she seemed to be in the movies was because he stayed under her. She appeared to be the babysitter, not the older sister.

I eventually got tired of watching Crystal get mistreated, ignored or yelled at. I took all of the movies into the backyard and burned them. They all showed footage of Crystal, but not my Crystal. She was depressed in all of them. Who in their right mind would want to watch that?

I tried to calm myself down, but the more I tried, the angrier I got. I hated myself for letting it happen. I spent the majority of the time thinking of ways that I could have prevented it. I thought about different things that I could have done. Finally it sunk in, it wasn't my fault at all. There was nothing that I could have done and that hurt worse.

Maria came home about six hours later. She wanted to give me plenty of time to watch the movies. She walked through the door with bags in her hands. Crystal had bags in her hands also. Maria knew from my eyes that I had been crying and was very upset. She sent Crystal upstairs to put away her new clothes.

"Don't worry," Maria said. "I spent my money."

"You know I'm not worried about money," I said.

"I know, just trying to get you to smile. What's wrong, baby? The DVDs weren't good?"

"Not at all," I said.

She walked up to me and gave me a kiss.

"Don't worry baby, you have the real thing now. You don't need the movies."

I kissed her on her left cheek, then on her right cheek, then on the lips.

"Yeah, Crystal and I both have the real thing now."

31

Two years had passed since we saw Anthony that day and everything is wonderful. Maria and I got married about two months after the meeting with Anthony. The wedding was short, but she loved it anyway.

Maria is pregnant again. She had my first son about eight months ago and now she is baking the next one. Crystal was so excited when Maria had the first baby that she made us set his crib up in her room. When Crystal found out that she was pregnant again, she started to rearrange her room to make way for the next one.

Crystal is growing up fast. She entered womanhood a week after she turned twelve. Crystal handled it well, I guess. Maria had to help her with all of that because I was truly lost.

Crystal is doing well in school also. She is making straight A's and is very proud to do it. She hasn't had any problems in school, no fighting at all. She turned into a model student.

I have calmed down a lot, too. The family that I have makes me control my anger. I can't believe the connection we have. Every time a bad day was about to come up, Crystal would have a dream. She would tell me to stay home that day or not go to a particular place. I don't work, but I normally go out to exercise or take the little man out for the day. Crystal has a strange connection with me, but she keeps me safe, so I never argue with her. This day was no different.

"Five minutes," I shouted. I grabbed my keys and my coat.

Crystal ran down the stairs. "I'm ready and so his he," she said, holding David in her arms. He always clung to her and she clung to him, but we made sure that we didn't push him on her. We let Crystal do her own thing, but she spent the majority of her free time with me or Maria, or David. Crystal loved her family and wasn't shy about it.

"Where is Maria?" I asked.

"Mom is upstairs putting on her face," Crystal said as she looked in the refrigerator to get the baby food.

I smiled because she called Maria her mom. She had been calling her mom since before we got married, but it was still special when I heard it. She really loved Maria and every time she called her mom, it confirmed it.

I remember the first time Maria heard it; she cried for about six hours. She smiled all day and hugged Crystal repeatedly. I think that she will remember that more than anything else in her life, even more than when our son or the next child calls her mom. They are going to do it because they're supposed to; Crystal does it because she wants to. Maria earned that title of mom and Crystal lets her know everyday.

I walked over to the steps and yelled, "Woman, let's go!"

Maria yelled back, "Don't mess with me, boy! I am tired and pregnant and don't feel like doing anything."

"That is why you are putting on your face, right?" I asked.

Maria started to walk down the stairs and said, "Well, I have to look good for you."

"You always look good," I replied as she reached the bottom step. I gave her a kiss on the lips. I hadn't seen her in over thirty minutes and I missed her.

Like clockwork, the sound came from the kitchen. "Yuck!" Crystal said.

Maria and I laughed. "Will that ever go away?" Maria asked.

"I don't think so," I said.

Maria walked around the corner and into the kitchen. She gave Crystal a hug and a kiss, then kissed Little Man on his forehead.

I followed Maria around the corner. "Hey, where is my kiss?" I asked.

"I already gave you your kiss," Maria said.

I poked my lip out like a child. Maria walked over to me and kissed me again.

"You big baby," she said.

"Yuck," Crystal said, laughing.

"How do you think David got here?" Maria asked, pointing at Little Man in Crystal's arms.

It was amazing the difference one person could make. Eight years ago, I had an argument because of that statement. Now, I heard nothing but laughter in the kitchen when that statement was made.

"Hey Dad, you have to stay home today," Crystal said.

"Have to stay home?" I asked. "David and I were going to the mall to check out the ladies."

Maria turned around and said, "Excuse me. Don't be trying to use my son as bait for those little hoochies."

Crystal laughed and continued, "It doesn't feel right, you know."

We left the house shortly after that. Maria went to work. I took Crystal to school and returned home with David.

We stayed in the house all day playing. He had every toy imaginable. He crawled all around the house with me chasing him and I ran around the house with him chasing me. He laid down about noon and went to sleep. As soon as I put him in his crib, the phone rang.

I ran into my bedroom and answered it. "Hello," I said, jumping across the bed to answer the phone.

"She is scaring me," Maria said.

"What happened?" I asked.

"Two men were arrested at the mall today. They tried to kidnap this little kid while his mother shopped. One of the guys grabbed him right out of the stroller while the other one looked out. When the mother realized what was going on, she ran after the man with her son. The lookout guy chased the mother, caught up to her and attacked her. He beat her until the mall security pulled him off of her. They caught the other guy in the parking lot."

I shook my head and said, "You know I would have killed them."

"Yeah, I do, and I think Crystal knew it too. Jim, you can't leave the house - ever."

I laughed and asked, "Ever?"

"I don't want anything to happen to you. What if they would have taken David? What if you would have been there and killed those guys? What would happen to us? I can't live without you and I know Crystal doesn't want to lose you again," Maria said with panic in her voice.

"Calm down baby, I am not going anywhere."

"I know. I just don't want to lose you."

"You won't. I am here to stay."

"You better be. Well, I have to go get back to work. I love you."

"I love you, too."

I hung up the phone and walked back downstairs. I sat on the couch and watched television until Crystal came home from school. As soon as she hit the door, David woke up. She dropped her book bag by the front door and ran upstairs to grab him. She walked back downstairs with him in her arms. I grabbed him from her and gave her a kiss.

"How was school?" I asked.

"Fine. I got an A on my test."

"That is good, sweetie."

Crystal walked to the front door to grab her book bag, then came back into the kitchen to do her homework. She pulled her books out of her book bag. She sat down, cracked them open and began to write.

"Hungry?" I asked.

"Yes," she said. "Can you make some of your chicken?"

I cooked the best chicken under the sun and she loved it.

"Can I ask you a question?" I asked.

"Sure," Crystal said, putting her pencil down and looking at me.

"What did you dream last night?"

She closed her eyes for a minute and tried to picture what she dreamed.

"Your eyes changed colors again. You looked regular, but your eyes were those wolf eyes again and the cage door was open. It was pretty much the same dream I have from time to time. Why? What happened?"

"Two guys were arrested at the mall today. I guess it was a good thing that I stayed home."

Crystal smiled and agreed, "I guess so."

She picked her pencil up and started her homework again. I put David on the island in the kitchen as I prepared to cook. He just sat there. We had a couple of close calls before with him diving over the side, but he has learned just to sit and play with the salt and pepper shakers.

I cooked as Crystal finished her homework. Once we both finished, we all sat down and ate. A couple of hours later, Maria came home. She ate dinner, then we all relaxed together. She had work that she needed to finish, but she said that it had to wait because she was going to spend time with her family.

About nine o'clock, everyone started to get ready for bed. Crystal took her shower with me standing guard. I never took a shower when Crystal took a shower. Every time she went into the bathroom, I would stand at the bottom of the steps or just hang around the door.

Once she finished and got dressed, I put Little Man in his bed and Crystal into hers. Maria sat in the rocking chair because she could no longer lay on the floor, and I laid on the floor beside Crystal.

When Crystal and I first moved in, I would lay on the floor beside her at night. When I would awake in the morning, Maria would be sleeping right next to me. It got to the point where we never slept in our bed. When Maria got pregnant the second time, I bought her the rocking chair because she refused to sleep in our bed while I was in the room with Crystal. Crystal, being the sweetheart that she is, told me that I could sleep in my room, and not stay with her all night. So now we stay in the room until Crystal and David fall asleep, which they usually do, pretty fast.

That night was no different. They were asleep within thirty minutes. Maria and I went into our room after setting up the baby monitor.

I smacked her on the butt and said, "You murderer." I would call her that from time to time, just to get a reaction out of her.

"I didn't murder anyone. Let me ask you a question. Did you have anything to do with that cop?"

I pretended like I didn't know who she was talking about. "What cop?"

"You know what cop. Don't make me hurt you."

"Well, did you have something to do with Emily?"

Maria smiled hard, not really knowing what to say. "No," she said and tried to hold back whatever thoughts were running through her head.

I smiled back at her and stated, "Well, I had nothing to do with the cop."

She looked at me for a second, then said, "Well, I'm glad that we had nothing to do with it, aren't you?"

"I sure am," I replied.

We curled up in bed together and she fell asleep in my arms. I kissed her and began to fall asleep myself.

It's funny how life is. One person made my life unbearable and another person gave me a whole new reason to live. It's funny how much of a difference one person can make.

I also realized that everything has its reasons for happening. I couldn't have Crystal if I hadn't had Emily. I couldn't have Maria if Emily never took Crystal. I wouldn't have millions of dollars if I didn't go to jail. I wouldn't be an 'Untouchable' if Anthony hadn't ordered everyone to kill me. I wouldn't appreciate Paul if I had never met Scott. I couldn't enjoy peace if I never went through the war.... and I wouldn't enjoy love if I didn't truly understand what it meant to hate.

www.ingramcontent.com/pod-product-compliance
Lightning Source LLC
Chambersburg PA
CBHW030326020726
47493CB00004B/1178